United Reign

Valentino Empire Series, Book 3

Kylie Kent

United Reign
Book 3
Valentino Empire

KYLIE KENT

Come and check out my website and join my mailing list to stay up to date and gain access to bonus materials.
Website & Newsletter: https://www.kyliekent.com/

If you want early access to everything, yes everything come and join my Patreon Group Kylie Kent Patreon

Want to be involved in discussions and have access to tons of give-aways? Join my readers group on Facebook Kylie's Steam Room

Facebook: @kyliekent2020
Instagram Follow: @author_kylie_kent_

Ebook ISBN 13: 9780645257243
Paperback ISBN: 9781922816061

Cover illustration by
Stacy Garcia - Graphics By Stacy

Editing services provided by
Kat Pagan – https://www.facebook.com/PaganProofreading

To Nate: Thank you for choosing me to be united in life with you. Xx

Chapter One

I *didn't know, T...*

Fucking Al Donatello's words repeat over and over in my head the whole trip back home. Fuck him and his fucked-up declaration. How the fuck did my mother do this? How is Al Donatello my father? I'm a Valentino. I'm not a fucking Donatello. Everything I know is Valentino.

I'm your father.

Fuck this. I need a goddamn drink. Unwrapping a sleeping Holly's arms from around me, I make my way out of the bedroom and into the lounge area of the jet. As soon as the seat belt signs dimmed, I brought Holly back into the bedroom and closed ourselves off from everyone. I'm not in the mood to be around anyone else. I've been waking Holly every two hours like the doctor instructed, and every time I do, I feel like shit all over again. She blinks back at me, confused. *Scared.* And then starts crying again. It takes her at least an hour to get back to sleep.

And here I am, stuck with that fucker's words in my fucking head, while Holly is suffering because I took her somewhere I never should have. I'll never forgive myself for bringing her to Donatello's estate. I don't expect her to ever forgive me either.

Neo looks up as I grab a bottle and a glass from the bar. He stands, walks over, and follows suit—pouring himself one as well. "How's she doing?" he asks, looking towards the back of the jet where Holly's tucked away in bed.

"Fucked up beyond repair," I say, tipping my head back. Is she really beyond repair? Have I managed to break the one good fucking thing I had in my life?

"She's tougher than you're giving her credit for, T. She will come out on the other side of this."

"Let's hope you're right." Another shot of whiskey slides down my throat. I don't even feel the burn I was seeking.

"How are you doing? You know, it might not be true... Your mother could have been talking shit, or maybe he's just mistaken—*heard her wrong.*"

We haven't spoken about what Donatello said. Neo was there, witnessed the whole damn thing. If it's true, that makes my cousin the rightful heir to the Valentino Empire. If it's true, I'm not even a Valentino. The one thing I've always been certain of. The thing that has literally shaped my entire existence—that's been an indisputable fact since the moment I was born. *I was the Valentino heir.* I would lead the family one day. My father drilled it into me every chance he got. I don't answer Neo, and instead, I take the bottle and the glass back to the bedroom.

My mother stops me along the way. "Theo, how's Holly?" I glare at her, and she flinches back from my stare. *Good.* I'd never actually hurt her, but fuck, I'm pissed as hell at the woman right now. Her face pales and her hands shake. "You know? He told you, didn't he?"

I see the truth in her eyes, the worry etched across her face. "The real question is: *why the fuck didn't you?*" I storm past her seat. I can't deal with her right now. I quietly enter the bedroom. Holly is still sleeping. Just as I'm about to shut the door, Neo shoves his way into the room. "If you wake her up, I'll fucking shoot you," I hiss at him.

He glances at the bed, and I see something unreadable flash in his eyes. "Fine, but you are not going through this shit alone, T. You wanna hit someone, wanna take your anger out on someone, then hit me. I can take it."

"What I want is for you to get my fucking mother off this plane, in a town car, and far away from me. I can't look at her right now. I have to take care of Holly. I can't handle this shit, the implications, any of it... On top of that, my wife comes first."

"She's tough, T. Much tougher than you think. She will get through this. What exactly is your plan when we get back to New York? Pretty sure the other families know by now... Word's probably gotten out that their little scheme—whatever the fuck that shit was all about—didn't go as planned."

"I don't give a fuck about their fucking plans. They sent me on a suicide mission; you and I both know that. The question is *why*?"

"You think they knew? About Donatello? They could have felt threatened, with you being the crowned prince and all now."

"I'm not the fucking crowned prince. Get that shit out of your head. I don't want anything to do with Donatello. My father died. You were there; you saw it."

"What's going on?" Holly's groggy voice has both of us snapping our heads back. I walk over to the bed and sit next to her, pulling her into my arms.

"Nothing, dolcezza. Go back to sleep." I kiss her forehead, on the side that isn't swollen. Seeing her like this makes me want to shed more fucking blood.

"Holly, how you holding up?" Neo asks.

"I'm... okay." Her words don't offer either of us any

reassurance. It's obvious that she's anything but *okay* right now.

"Right, I'll be out there. We're landing soon, so... you'll have to come and belt up. You know where to find me if you need anything, Hol." With that, Neo walks back out into the main cabin, sending one final glare in my direction. What the fuck I did to piss him off, I have no fucking idea. Nor do I care at the moment.

"How are you really doing, Holly?" I tilt her face up so I can see her eyes.

"I don't know. I feel... numb. But I just... I killed someone, T. I should feel something. Remorse, regret, sadness, anger. I don't know, but I just feel *numb*."

"Never regret fighting for yourself, Holly. You didn't *kill* anyone. You put down a fucking monster. That's not taking a life; that's sending a demon back to hell. What you did was community service, really."

"Maybe," she says pensively. "Are you going to leave again? I mean, when we get back home, what's going to happen?"

"I'm never leaving again, dolcezza. When we get home, we are going to lock ourselves in our apartment and not come out for weeks. I want uninterrupted time with you, just me and you."

"I like that plan."

"Come on, let's go sit down so we can get to it sooner."

The moment I enter the foyer of the penthouse, I smell it. *Rotting flesh.* I pull Holly behind me and have my gun drawn within seconds. Neo stands in front of me, attempting to push me backwards. "Get her out of here, T." He shoves against my chest. "NOW!" he screams when I don't move.

"What's happening? What's that smell?" Holly asks, trying to step around me.

"Neo, take her to the car. I'll be down in a minute." I throw the order at him, intent on finding out what's waiting for me.

"No, both of you stop talking about me like I'm not even here. I'm not going anywhere without you, T. So either you're coming to the car, or I'm staying right here." Holly manages to make her way beside me, somehow twisting out of the grip I had on her arm.

"Stay here, both of you." Neo walks farther into the apartment.

I'm torn over what to do. I want to follow him to see what the fuck is going on. But I also don't want to leave Holly behind, or let her see whatever's waiting for me just around the corner. And I know if I follow Neo, there is no way Holly won't *follow me.* And the last thing I want is to expose her to whatever hell is mere feet away. I should turn around, get her the fuck out, and take her to one of the family's safe houses.

"What the fuck?!" My cousin's voice travels down the hall. Instinct has me running towards him. I stop as soon as I cross the threshold into the bedroom. I see a pale-faced Neo... and the scene that's made him look like he's about to lose his breakfast.

On the bed, on our fucking marital bed, are two human carcasses. A male and a female. They've been here a while, the decomposing bodies a clear representation of me and my wife. Whoever did this wanted them to look like *us*. The woman's a redhead... fuck! They wanted us to find this. They wanted me to know they could get to us. *Get to her*.

The bastards sent a fucking message, and it's been received. *Loud and fucking clear*. They want a war. A war I'm going to fucking win.

"Oh my God!" Holly's gasp shakes me from my internal rage.

"Dolcezza, it's okay. It'll be okay." I wrap my arms around her and bury her head into my chest. I don't want her looking at this. I don't want her anywhere near this fucking shit. Not anymore. And not again.

Chapter Two

Holly

I t's been two weeks since we landed back in New York. Nothing is the same though. I'm not the same person I was when I left. Theo's not the same person either; he's turning into someone I don't recognize. Then again, so am I.

I can barely close my eyes without reliving the moment when I took someone else's life. Out of anger.

Revenge. I could have let Donatello handle it. I could have run out of the room and not looked back. But, instead, everything in me wanted to hurt that man. I wanted to make sure he'd never hurt another woman like he wanted to hurt me, like he did hurt me. I don't regret what I did. No, my nightmares are not about killing him. They're about what would have happened if Donatello hadn't come into the room to help me... if he hadn't intervened. Add that to the scene welcoming us back to the city... The bodies. The stench. It all just won't leave my head. I'm jumping at every damn shadow. Every sound.

As much as I'm trying hard not to show how affected I am, Theo sees straight through my façade. He's said so... countless times. But he's stressed; he's barely getting three hours of sleep a night. I know something is going on. I can feel the tension in the air. I've overheard conversations between my husband and Neo. Things I'm not meant to hear. A war is coming. But every time I ask either of them about it, I get the same vague answers: It's nothing for you to worry about... We have everything under control...

If it were nothing for me to worry about, then why are there so many more men in suits roaming around us than I've ever seen before? Armed men. And why has my husband had a distant, detached look in his eyes for the last two weeks?

I want to help him. I want to do whatever I can to make this situation better, though I'm pretty sure I've just been making it worse. I'm something else he has to protect and look after. If I wasn't here, would it be easier for him to fight whatever this is? Reilly has been begging me to return home to Sydney. She doesn't know what's going on here. I haven't told her what happened in Italy, but she's aware something happened. She knows I'm not okay right now.

I've considered taking her up on her offer, but every time the thought comes to mind, I immediately dismiss it. The idea of being that far away from T again sends an indescribable ache to my heart. Would my life be easier if I went back to Sydney? Yes. Would I be safer back in Sydney? Also, yes. But I wouldn't be living. I would rather stay, stand beside my husband, and fight through the depths of hell before ever going on without him. Because a life without T would not be a life at all.

It's literally my worst nightmare. I know because I lived it, just a few weeks ago when I thought Theo had been blown up in that house. For three days, he let me think he was dead... and for what? Nothing has been resolved from what I can tell. He still has enemies coming after him. After me. Everything we've been through over the last couple of months is only the kindling on the fire that's about to blaze through this town.

I need to find a way to get T to be present. Here. With me. To get him to confide in me, let me take away some of his worries and help him. We're a team. We should be united in this fight. This isn't his war. It's ours.

With renewed determination, I jump out of bed. A bed I've been lying around in for weeks, not doing much of anything at all. I head into the bathroom first. I need to handle some much-needed maintenance. When I look in the mirror, it's no wonder T has been treating me with kid gloves. I look like a mess. I don't even recognize the woman staring back at me.

After spending an hour in the shower, I blow dry my hair out, and for the first time in two weeks, I put some makeup on. Well, I apply some mascara and lip gloss, but that counts. Now, to find something to wear. I want Theo to notice me. And not for being the frightened, scared, helpless woman I've been for two weeks. I want him to look at me with desire. I want him to want me again. I'm about to pull a dress off the hanger when a thought comes to mind. What if he doesn't want me anymore? After what happened in Italy, does he see me as damaged goods?

I collapse to the floor of the closet. I'm in a house I don't know. Surrounded by people I don't know. Waiting for a threat I know nothing about... After Sonnie, I've avoided getting close to any of the men working for Theo. It's easier to not learn their names, to not know if they have families who will miss them when they take another bullet meant for me. We haven't even had a funeral for him yet. Where is his body? Were his loved ones told what happened to him?

I bury my head into my knees, my tears falling freely down my cheeks. So much for my five minutes of bravado. My hands pull at the ends of my hair. I feel like I'm losing my damn mind. My thoughts are jumping all over the place, and there's an endless list of questions left unanswered because I can't bring myself to ask them.

I couldn't tell you if I was sitting in the closet for a minute or an hour. The instant I felt a pair of strong arms wrap around me and tug me from the floor, I was drawn out of my thoughts. I buried my head into his chest and inhaled the familiar musky scent.

"It's okay. I've got you, dolcezza." His voice is hoarse, choked up with emotion.

"But do you still want me?" And I instantly regret letting the question slip from my lips.

T pulls back, lifting my chin until my watery eyes meet his dark ones. "There isn't a second that goes by that I don't want you, Holly. You are my whole fucking world." He sighs and then leans in and kisses my forehead while smoothing my hair back. "I know I've been... preoccupied since we've returned. But I never want you to question your place here. I'm sorry if I've made you feel unwanted. I fucking want you. If I could get away with having you handcuffed to me 24/7, I fucking would."

"I'm sorry. I shouldn't have said anything," I whisper. What was I thinking? I'm meant to be helping him, not adding to the burden he's already carrying.

"Yeah, you should have. It's not your fault if you felt unwanted; it's mine."

"That's not true. It's just... we haven't... Well, you know we haven't done... it since coming back home."

T quirks an eyebrow at me. "Sex, Holly. You can say the word. I've heard much worse come out of that pretty little mouth before." He laughs. "I don't want you to feel like we have to have sex. After what happened, I just thought that maybe you'd need some time."

He thought I'd need some time? "What I need is for you to touch me, T. I need to lose myself in you."

I see the lust in his eyes. He smirks as he trails his fingers along the inside of my thigh, pushing the towel upward. "You want me to touch you, dolcezza? Where?"

"Everywhere," I moan as his fingers reach higher, lightly brushing over my pussy lips.

T jumps to his feet, and the next minute, I land flat on my back on the bed. "Don't move," he says as he walks into the closet. Where the bloody hell is he going? He doesn't leave me waiting long, however, returning with two black silk ties in his hand. He kneels on the bed, a knee strategically positioned between my thighs. My breath catches as he leans forward and growls into my ear, "Arms above your head, dolcezza."

I don't hesitate to comply. My arms practically fly

above my head, following his instruction as my body tingles with anticipation.

"Good girl." His teeth graze my earlobe as he wraps one of the ties around both of my wrists. He then secures it to the rail on the bedhead. I instinctively pull on the restraints but get nowhere.

"Were you a boy scout?" I ask. He clearly knows how to tie a good knot.

"No." His lips trail down my neck and along my collarbone, before he grabs my chin between his fingers and slams his lips down on mine. His tongue forcefully invades my mouth. We duel for control for only a minute, until I submit to his demanding, rough strokes. He pulls away. "Fuck, I've missed this mouth," he says. Then, he straightens and retrieves the other tie he discarded beside my head. I pull on my wrists again, but there's no use. I'm not getting out of this. I'm at his mercy.

"Where'd you learn to tie knots like that if you weren't a boy scout?" I ask, tugging on the bindings again.

T looks at me and smirks. "Some things are best left unanswered, dolcezza. Now lie still." He places the silk tie over my eyes and lifts my neck slightly, somehow managing to secure the material behind my head. I feel his breath on my throat... my ear. My chest rises and falls rapidly, and a light sweat coats my skin, causing a chill to travel along my spine and goosebumps to accompany it. "You have no idea how badly I want to bury my cock so far into your tight little pussy and fuck you into tomorrow. I want you to feel me in every little movement your body makes."

"Yes, that. Do that, T. Now!" I yell.

"Tsk, tsk, tsk. I remember someone begging me to touch them all over. So that's what I'm going to do. I'm going to lick, suck, and kiss every goddamn inch of this delicious fucking body of yours."

I release a mix between a groan and a moan when I feel his mouth close over my neck, just under my ear. His teeth dig in as he sucks, only to let go and lick the same spot, the sensation oddly soothing against the ache of the bite. I don't know how I'll survive whatever he has planned. I'm on fire, my core is pulsing with the need to feel him inside me, and my juices are already leaking down my inner thighs.

At the realization, my cheeks heat up and I know I'm flush.

Chapter Three

Having Holly tied up and sprawled out for me is an aphrodisiac like no other. Her body is fucking perfection. As I make my way down her torso, licking, biting, and sucking on every inch of her silky-smooth skin, I can't help but thank God for the gift that is my wife. There is so much I want to do with this body, so many experiences I want to give her. To be able to offer her the kind of pleasure she's never had before. That's what I want to do... I want to bury myself so deep within her soul that I become part of hers.

As I reach the apex of her thighs, I stop and jump up. "Hold that thought. Don't move." I laugh as I walk into the closet for a second time.

"What the hell, T? Where'd you go? Don't you dare leave me here!" she yells, struggling against her restraints.

"Holly, I'm never leaving you." I climb back onto the bed, placing the objects I retrieved next to her. Leaning in, I take her lips, nibbling on the bottom one before forcing my tongue inside her mouth. "Mmm, you always taste so fucking good."

"Maybe you should never stop tasting me then?" Holly questions.

"Don't worry, I won't." I offer her one last peck on the lips. "Do you trust me, Holly?" I ask.

"More than anyone."

"Good, because what I'm about to do to you, what I'm about to give you, show you, you're going to need to hold on to that trust. Believe that I'm going to make you feel things you've never felt before." I start making my way down her body, settling myself between her legs.

"Mmm, what?"

"Shh, don't question. Don't think. Just feel, dolcez-za." I run my tongue up the length of her slit. As much as I want to dive in and drown in her, feast like the starving man I am, I want to drive her out of her mind with need more. I take my time, spreading her lips with my fingers as I slowly trail my tongue up her center before twisting it around her hardened bud. I grab the bottle of lube with my free hand and pop the top. Squirting a little on my fingers, I rub circles around her back entrance.

"Ah, T, I'm not sure..." Holly's words trail off when I insert my finger and suck on her clit at the same time. "Oh, fuck!" she screams as her body tenses up and clenches.

"Relax, Holly. Trust me," I say before slowly stroking my finger in and out of her ass while licking and sucking on her clit.

"Oh God, T. Don't stop. Oh my God..." These are the sounds I live to hear. I add another digit and start to twirl them around, stretching her out. Once I feel she's about to come, I stop and pull back my hand. "What, T? No, don't stop. I was so close," she growls—yes, growls.

I laugh. "Don't worry, dolcezza, I'm not stopping. Just... stepping things up a notch," I say, picking up the plug and covering it in lube.

"What does that mean?"

"You'll see. Now, I'm going to need you to relax and hold still." I slowly push the tip of the plug into her hole.

"What is that, T? No, I don't think I can do this." She's clenched up, panicked at the unknown.

Leaning over, I whisper into her ear, "Puoi farlo. Credimi, ti farà sentire bene. Hai solo bisogno di rilassarti. Sei così fottutamente sexy in questo momento, Holly." I feel her body start to relax, so I nudge the plug in deeper as I repeat my words in English. "You can do this. Trust me, this is going to feel good. You just need to relax. You are so fucking sexy right now, Holly."

Once the sleek black toy is fully seated, I pick up the controller and turn it to the lowest setting, smirking as I watch the shock appear on Holly's face. "Wait... what the bloody hell is that? Oh... oh God!" Her hips are moving, searching, squirming.

"This is going to be tight," I say, lining up my cock with the entrance of her pussy. I drive in slowly, feeling the vibrations humming through her body. "Fuck me, you feel amazing, dolcezza."

"Holy crap, I feel so full. T, don't stop." Holly's hips are moving in time with my thrusts. She clamps her legs around my waist, linking her ankles together behind me. I let her set the speed and pace. It only takes minutes before she's convulsing around my cock, milking me for everything I have to give her.

"Fuck!" I grunt as I fall onto the bed next to her. I reach down and gently remove the plug before lifting the blindfold and smirking at her post-orgasm, blissed-out face. "Good?" I question, raising an eyebrow. I already know she just came harder than she ever has.

"Uh-huh," she answers breathlessly. We lie there for a few minutes, allowing the oxygen to return to our lungs, before the reality of our lives comes crashing back down on us.

"T, what's going to happen now?"

"Now, I'm going to run a bath and enjoy washing you from head to toe."

"Okay."

I know that's not the answer she was looking for, but fuck, what the fuck am I supposed to tell her? That we're currently at war with three other fucking mafia families? That I'm scared I'm actually in a fight I can't win this time? That everything I thought I was... was nothing but a fucking lie?

We've been soaking in the tub for thirty minutes. I've never felt so at ease. Yet, at the same time, tension thickens the air. I know Holly has questions she wants to ask. I also know she's trying her hardest to hold back from verbalizing them. "Just ask," I prompt, rubbing my hands up and down her arms, her body resting against my chest.

She tilts her head back to look at me. "Ask what?"

"Whatever it is that's on your mind. I can tell you want to ask something, dolcezza. Just ask."

"I don't... Okay." She sits up and spins around in the tub to face me. The loss of her body against mine should be a fucking crime. I don't like it. I wait for her to speak though. As much as I want to pull her back into my arms, I don't. "What's going to happen now... with your family? The other families? Have you thought about talking to your mum? To Donatello? Where are we going to live? Are we ever going to go back to your apartment? What about my apartment? I still have all my things there... What about my job? I should start looking for another teaching job, right?"

"Dolcezza, take a breath. That's a lot of questions. Have you just been walking around this whole time with all these things on your mind?"

"Among others." She nods.

"Okay, let's start with the easy ones. Your job? That's up to you. If it were up to me, I'd have you locked in a tower somewhere forever." I raise my finger when she opens her mouth to argue. "But I know that's not a realistic option, at least not for you." Taking a breath, I refill our wine glasses and hand Holly hers.

"Thank you."

"If you want to work, Holly, I can find you a position in one of my companies," I offer.

"And what? Teach your employees how to read? How to multiply? Thanks, but I think I'll stick to third-graders."

"You'd be surprised how many of them could learn something from you, dolcezza."

"Doubtful. What are you going to do about your mum? She's been calling every day, T. You can't ignore her forever."

"I can. You couldn't, because you're a nice person.

Me, I'm an asshole. I absolutely could pretend she doesn't exist."

"You're not an asshole, T. You're hurt and understandably so. But I want you to try to resolve this. I happen to love your mother. I want our children to have her around, so we need to find a way to work through this. Ignoring it doesn't make it go away..."

"She lied to me my whole fucking life, Holly. My father, did he even know? Fucking hell, how can someone do that?" The more I think about it, the more I get myself worked up again. I can't forgive and forget, or do some kumbaya shit and simply work through this with her. My whole life was a fucking lie.

"I don't know, and neither do you. It's something you work on. You ask her the questions only she can answer. I'm sure she had her reasons, although there may not be any excuse. We weren't there. We don't know what happened."

What I don't know... is how to respond to that. I'm not sure if I'm ready to forgive my mother. Just as I go to open my mouth to respond, the unmistakable sound of bullets tearing through the air fills the void. "Fuck! Get up!" I yell, pulling Holly out of the water. I grab the dressing gown off the hook on the door and wrap it around her, before I yank a pair of sweatpants out of the hamper and throw them on.

Opening the door, I scan the bedroom. There's no one in sight. Tugging Holly behind me, I place a finger to my mouth, gesturing for her to be quiet. The shouts are muffled, the gunfire distant—it's coming from outside. Walking into the closet, I hit the button that opens the back wall to a hidden hallway.

I have one thing on my mind: getting Holly the fuck out of here.

Chapter Four

Holly

What the hell is going on? I want to ask Theo, but the tension radiating off him keeps my mouth shut tight, and I blindly follow him and his every instruction. There's a secret door in the closet. I'm not sure why I'm surprised—all of T's homes are like Hogwarts with secret doors and passageways everywhere. Yes, these are the insane thoughts running rampant in my mind as T pulls me through what looks like a hallway. It's dark, damp, and musty. But at least I can't hear the gunshots anymore. "Who's shooting at us?" I ask him, breaking the silence.

His steps halt, and he turns to cup my face with his palms. "Not us, dolcezza. Me. Don't worry about it. I'm getting you out of here. I won't let anything happen to you—I swear it." He drops his hands and grips one of mine again, turning towards wherever it is this tunnel leads. I pull on his arm until he stops.

"If they're shooting at you, then they're shooting at me too. Because I'm nothing without you, Theo. I have a right to know who the bloody hell thinks they can take you away from me." My rage is rising to the surface, replacing the initial fear. I can't lose him again. I won't lose him again. My blood might be at its boiling point right now, but T is grinning like a damn lunatic. "Why are you smiling? This isn't a laughing matter, Theo."

"You're incredibly fucking sexy when you get all protect my man, Holly. I want nothing more than to push you up against this wall, spread those creamy thighs of yours, and impale your pussy on my cock." He sighs. "But I can't do that right now, because I need to get you out of here. I need to clean up this mess. And I need to find Neo and make sure my men are still fucking breathing. But most of all, I need you to hold on to that fire and help me keep you safe."

Well, what the hell do I say to that? "Maybe I was wrong about your Hallmark career. You should go into politics, T. That was one hell of a speech. But you should know I'd follow you anywhere without all the fancy words." When he stands there staring at me with his eyebrows drawn, I urge him back into action. "Come on, what are we waiting for? Move." I push him to start walking again.

"I fucking love you, Holly," he says, quickening his pace. I have to almost jog to keep up with him.

Chapter Five

Every day, I fall more and more in love with Holly. I never thought a love like this was possible. I thought it was the kind of shit people made up. A fairy tale to sell children into thinking there was something big and great in the world, just waiting for them to find it. The pursuit of love really is life's greatest treasure hunt. Because when you find it, you fucking treasure it. You protect it with everything you have.

And that's what I'm doing right now. I'm protecting my treasure from the darkness of my fucked-up existence. I should be up there fighting next to my men. I should be safeguarding my family. And a few months ago, I would have been. But now, my wife comes before anyone and anything else.

We're almost at the door that connects the brownstone (where we are staying temporarily) to Helena's café. I always thought Neo was a paranoid bastard when he put this tunnel in a few years back. But now, I get it and I'm fucking thankful he did. Our current residence belongs to his family. It was purchased in his sister's name—the same girl who's been missing for years. No one's supposed to know we're here.

How the fuck did they find us? How many fuckers do I need to slaughter today? Whoever thinks they can shoot up my house and walk away is fucking dreaming. I will find each and every one of those bastards and fucking end them. Painfully. I smile at the thought of having the faceless assholes strung up in my warehouse, stripped of everything they thought they were.

After five minutes of navigating the dark tunnel, we reach its end. Opening the door a crack, I look through to the kitchen. Everything appears to be operating as normal, with staff going about their daily business. We get inquisitive looks as I drag Holly towards the back office.

Closed in the small room, I can see everything. My

eyes scan the live camera feed. Helena is greeting and serving customers, as she is known to do. "Wait here." I kiss Holly's forehead before shutting her inside and heading to the dining area.

"What's wrong? What happened? Where's Neo?" Helena asks as she rushes forward and tugs me into the kitchen.

"The house got shot up. I don't know. I didn't have a chance to grab my phone. I need yours."

"You ran? You ran out and left my brother there to defend himself?" she yells.

"Watch who the fuck you're talking to, Helena. I'm about to head back there. I need your fucking phone now, and I need you to keep Holly here until I return. Think you can do that?" I growl out, annoyed at her tone and accusations. I hold my palm open in front of her. She pulls her phone from the pocket of her apron and slams it into my hand. "Thank you. Tell my wife I'll be back for her and not to move until I am."

"What? You didn't tell her that you're leaving her here? Great, let me go deal with the fallout of that conversation. Thanks, T," Helena hisses at my retreating form as I run through the door to the tunnel.

The house is eerily quiet. Tiptoeing along the hall and down the stairs, I draw my gun. Ready. On edge. As I make my way through the brownstone, I hear him before I see him. My cousin, quietly cursing and promising someone a brutally gruesome death. Fuck, I know that tone. I've heard those promises many times before. Seen them delivered too. Whoever he's speaking to has royally fucked up—that's for sure.

Rounding the corner, my heart stops. Sitting in the middle of the kitchen is Neo. Tied to a fucking chair. Blood runs like a leaky faucet down his temple. His shredded shirt shows red marks all over his chest. I don't think. I don't have time to consider my actions. The hot end of my barrel rises to eye-level, and I aim at the fucker closest to Neo. And then, one by one, all three men (who were stupid enough to have their backs to a fucking doorway) fall to the ground.

"What the fuck took you so long?" Neo grunts as he fights against the ropes still holding him in place.

I take a knife out of the butcher's block on the bench and free his wrists from behind. "What the fuck happened to you? How'd you let them get you in this chair?" I know Neo can handle himself; he wouldn't have gone down easily. How these three goons got the better of him, I'll never understand.

"Where the fuck are your clothes?" he grunts, ignoring my question as he starts searching through the cabinets.

I look down and realize I'm still only wearing a pair of sweatpants. Then I remember I put Holly in a fucking dressing gown before leaving her in a café full of people. "I was in the fucking bath. I took Holly through the tunnel and left her at Helena's."

"Is she okay? Holly?"

I know it shouldn't bother me how close the two became when I wasn't there. He did protect her after all, helped her through a rough time. A time that never should have fucking happened. But fuck, it pisses me off. Jealousy is not a feeling I've ever had to deal with before. "She's fine." I turn around, surveying the fucking destruction left behind. "What the fuck happened here?"

"Good question. How'd these assholes know about this place?"

"Come on, let's find out what the damage is, then we'll go paint the fucking city red."

Twenty dead. Twenty of my fucking men died today, and for what? Greed. Greedy fucking sick bastards, who ain't too happy I've put a stop to the gravy train steamrolling through my city. They think running kids, selling fucking little girls, is going to fly with me? Fuck that. I'm all for making a quick turnover, but even the devil himself has some fucking limits.

Neo and I have hit back hard. We don't need a team of men to hurt these families. I already know their weaknesses, know every-fucking-thing they hold dear.

It's not their wives and children. No, I don't need to stoop to that level to hurt them. I'm gunning for what will pain them the most. What they value above all else. Their fucking money. This is the last stop of the night. I want to get home (wherever the fuck that is right now) and I want to get back to Holly.

"You ready for this?" Neo asks as he reloads and straps extra magazines to himself.

Pulling the slide back, I release it again and chamber a round. "Yep, let's do this."

The crazy fucker doesn't bother to wait for me; he kicks in the door to the club and starts firing. On the outside, this place looks like a respectable establishment. However, on the inside, it's nothing but a shell of a building, full of equipment and paper. This is where the Garzo family prints their money. Billions of dollars' worth of product is housed within these walls. Their money laundering business is their most profitable. That's why we're burning it down.

We've already hit the other two families. The explosion of five warehouses full of weapons and ammo was probably seen all the way on the west coast —it was that fucking big. But this place? I knew Beno would be here. He's a controlling fuck and a creature of habit. He also holds the answers to the questions running on repeat in my head. Questions I'm going to have answered tonight.

I search the area. It's like a ghost town. Most of the men would have been sent out to deal with the destruction we caused down by the docks. I spot Beno sitting at a table, the shock on his face clear as day. Neo had the four men down before they could even blink. My cousin's quick, probably quicker than me, not that I'll ever fucking admit that to the cocky bastard.

"Well, look, boss. I think we found our man, here. And all alone too." Neo's voice is playful.

"Looks like it. You should be more careful, Beno. From what I hear, you've got yourself a line of enemies around this city, just waiting to take you out."

"You can't do shit to me, boy. I'm a fucking Don," the old man spits.

"Yeah, you see, I was raised to respect the rules of our forefathers. Blah, blah, blah. But that respect went out the fucking window when you and your pals sent me on a fucking suicide mission."

"We didn't. I don't have any idea what you're talking about."

"You know, I learned something while I was away. Italians drink a lot. And when they drink, they talk. Loose lips and all that. And, well, the names that kept coming up? Yeah, they were real interesting. Can you guess whose they were?" I walk around the room, placing bundles of dynamite in each of the corners. His beady eyes watch me, attempting to calculate how he can either talk or fight his way out of this. "No guesses, huh?" I say, turning back to the dead man. "Tell me, Beno. Why was it that you old bastards wanted to get rid of me?"

"We didn't. We don't," he says, and his delivery is almost believable.

"Yeah, you did," I retort. "Look, we can spend all night doing this, or we can get it over with quick. Your choice. But you should know, if we have to spend all night here, I'm going to be pissed. I have a wife waiting for me. And I don't like making her fucking wait." I nod my head to Neo while rolling up the sleeves of my shirt.

"You think you'll get away with this? You won't. They'll come for you, T. They'll come for her too. I hope you're ready to watch your whore of a wife get the treatment you deserve." At that, I see fucking red. The haze takes over. I don't think. I don't feel. I just do. I lay into him, landing hit after hit to his head.

"Fuck, T, stop! You're going to kill him before he can tell you what we need to know." Neo grunts with the effort it takes to pull me back. I look at Beno's face (or what's left of it) and he smiles. Fucking deranged bastard. He knew exactly what to say to get me to drop my focus. He wanted me to lose control, to end him sooner. Fuck that. No.

I tilt my head at him. "Neo, get the bag," I instruct while smirking at Beno, and the son of a bitch finally pales. I know the reputation I've garnered in our circle. And I know he knows he just poked the fucking crazy in me. My mind clears as I conjure up all the ways I'm going to make this fucker wish for the respite the flames of hell are sure to offer him.

Chapter Six

Holly

I hear Helena yelling at T through the closed door. Jumping up, I make out his silhouette in the darkness of the passageway leading back into the house. He left me here. That asshole actually left me here without saying goodbye. Helena turns around, her eyebrows drawn as she looks me up and down. I tighten the belt on the robe I'm wearing. The bathrobe I'm bloody wearing. I'm standing in a café barely clothed, and he left me here. I'm going to wring his pretty little neck when I see him. He's returning to the house. The same one that people were shooting at.

"Holly, let me make you a cup of tea. Wait in the office. I'll bring you some food too. I'm sure T will be back really soon," Helena says cautiously, as she eyes me like I'm a wild animal. And I guess, at the moment, I kind of am.

"No, I'm okay and when my husband does come back, you can tell him to go straight to hell. If he thinks for one minute I'm going to sit around waiting for him, well, he can just think again. Thanks, Helena. I'm sorry we barged in like this." I walk through the kitchen and into the café area.

"Wait! Where are you going?" Helena rushes after me.

"Home. Right after I stop at a Bottle-O." I push through the door, ignoring all the curious glares in my direction.

"Wait! I'll come with you. What's a Bottle-O?"

"A liquor store. I'm day drinking, and if you're coming with me, then so are you."

"Okay, I'm down. Fuck those boys and always thinking we'll just wait around for them like helpless little damsels."

I smile at her. I'm aware that I probably look like I just escaped the looney bin right now. I'm walking through the streets of New York in a bathrobe after all.

Conveniently, there is a bottle shop just a block away from my apartment, and that's where I'm heading.

"So, what's the plan? What's your choice of poison?" Helena asks.

"Oh, it's got to be tequila today." I smile at her, although I feel like doing anything but smiling right now.

My mind is whirling, and I can't shut it down. Where is T? Is he in trouble? Is he doing something reckless? Well, that one I can answer with a definitive yes. I'm pissed off at him, but at the same time, I just want to see his face. Mostly so I can slap it, but also because I need him to be okay. Maybe this whole mafia thing isn't really for me. I don't know how I can go through life, knowing he's out there somewhere and people are looking to kill him.

We walk the rest of the way in silence. Entering the liquor store, I pick up two bottles of tequila and head to the checkout. It's not until I get there that I realize I don't have a wallet. I don't have any money either. I didn't even bring my phone. I look to Helena. "Ah, I kind of don't have any cash on me," I say, embarrassed. The laugh that she lets out is loud and unashamed.

"Holly, you don't need cash. Tell him your name." She nods to the young guy at the register, who glances between us with panic on his face.

"Uh, hi. I'm Holly." I smile at him and look back to Helena.

"No, your full name, Holly."

"Ah, Holly Valentino," I say, my gaze landing on the guy again. His pupils instantly dilate and his face pales. I know I shouldn't, but I roll my eyes at the effect that name has on people. I wouldn't usually use it to my advantage, but today, I'm running low on options. "Look, I know this is... unconventional. But if you just let me take these two bottles, I give you my word I'll return tomorrow and pay for them."

"Oh, no. You can take them, Mrs. Valentino. No worries. You don't have to pay for them."

My eyebrows draw down. "I promise I'll return and pay for them. Thank you."

"Are you okay, Mrs. Valentino? Are you in some kind of trouble? Do you need help?" he asks me.

"Well, my husband's an asshole apparently, and I'm going to wring his neck when I see him. But other than that, I'm just peachy." I smile my sweetest smile.

The poor guy... If his eyes get any wider, I think his eyeballs might just fall right out of their sockets. "Um..." he stammers.

"It's fine. Forget you heard that," Helena says, pulling me out of the store while grabbing the bottles from my hands.

"You really shouldn't tell people T is an asshole." For a moment, I think she's joking. I mean, she has to be. But when I look at her face, it's stone-cold serious.

"Oh my God! You're serious right now? And why can't I tell people my husband's an ass when he most definitely is one."

"Well, I know that. You know that. But they—the

people around here—they idolize him, Holly. They won't take kindly to their king being disrespected."

"Well, apparently, I'm the queen, so I think that means I can do and say whatever I want. Let them all hate me... come at me. I really don't care. In fact, as soon as I get my hands on a phone, I'm calling Theo and telling him how much of an asshole I think he's being right now."

"Okay, come on. Let's go drink our sorrows away."

"So, did you have a plan on how you were going to get in?" Helena asks as we both stare at my locked apartment door.

"Obviously, I didn't think that far ahead." I scowl. Then I remember the landlord lives up on the top floor. "Wait, the landlord, he has to have spare keys, right?" Just as we're about to turn around and head back to the lift, the door opens and standing inside my apartment is probably one of the most beautiful women I've ever seen. I mean, I've never been tempted to switch teams, but bloody hell if anyone could convince me, it would be her. She's tall, tanned, slim. With the sort of cheekbones girls spend hours contouring to achieve. And those eyes, they're dark. But there's something so familiar about them too.

"I was wondering how long it takes people to open

a door," she says in a thick European accent. When neither Helena or I say anything, she speaks up again. "You are Holly, right? From the description my father gave me, I'd be able to pick you out of a lineup of redheads. But he underdelivered when it came to just how beautiful you were." She beams a perfect smile at me.

I pull myself out of my shock. "Who are you? And what are you doing in my apartment?"

"Mama, is that her? Is Aunt Holly here?" I hear a little voice ask from inside. I glance to Helena, who shrugs her shoulders but is also cautiously looking around the hallway like she's expecting the boogeyman to jump out at any moment.

"Sorry, I apologize. My name is Angelica Donatello. I believe you met my father in Italy a few weeks back, and I've recently come to learn that your husband, Theo, is my brother. I'd very much like to see him."

Theo has a sister? I remember he mentioned something briefly during a discussion about the whole paternity news he was just handed. Something about a niece, but the fact that he also had a sister didn't occur to me. He's struggling to accept that the man who raised him wasn't his biological father. I'm not too sure how he's going to deal with the fact that he has a sister looking for him. Right now though, I'm on a mission, a mission to forget everything with the aid of tequila.

"Huh, well, that makes two of us. When you find

him, tell him not to bother looking for me," I say as I walk past her and into the living room. "Also, why exactly are you in my apartment?"

I stop short when I come to a little girl. She can't be any older than eight. "Ah, it is you. Hello, my name is Isabella. But you can call me Izzy. I've never had an aunt before, so I'm very excited that I've got one now," the little girl rambles.

I bend down to meet her at eye-level. "Hi, Izzy. My name is Holly. I've never been an aunt before either, but I'm honored to be yours," I tell her. Then I straighten and glare over her head at her mother.

"Oh, right. Well, I was snooping, of course. I thought there might be a clue as to where I could find my brother."

"Well, he isn't here. Helena, I'm going to go shower and put some clothes on." I don't have it in me to deal with people right now. I just want to hide away. I want to restart the day and go back to when I was tied to the bed with T's head between my legs. Why does it feel like I'm living in a never-ending nightmare? "Izzy, it was great to meet you, sweetheart. But as you can see, I need to go get dressed." I smile at the blissfully oblivious little girl. I'd love to borrow just a bit of her innocence, to be in the dark when it came to the dangers lurking around every corner.

I head into the bathroom and lock the door. Everything looks the same, but I can sense she was in here. I feel violated, having this space searched by a stranger. I don't have a lot of personal things left in my apartment. I'm surprised I haven't just handed the keys back yet. I haven't been back here since we were married. I guess I just never gave it too much thought. Until today. Until I needed space.

I turn the faucet on and sit on the shower floor, letting the warm water wash over me. My mind whirls with thoughts, and I really bloody wish I brought one of those bottles of tequila in here with me. It doesn't take long for the tears to escape. "Why? Why is this happening? What do I do?"

I just need someone to tell me what I need to do. Where is T? I hate how much I need him. I hate how codependent I've become. And I hate how he can so easily leave me and go off, putting himself in danger, when I've begged him not to. But most of all, I hate that I'm wishing he were someone else right now. Someone with an ordinary life and an ordinary job, where his rivals don't carry automatic weaponry. Someone who's safe.

The little voice in my head reminds me that it's because of who he is that I fell in love with him. This deep, hidden part of me craves his darkness, thrives on it. I just haven't had time to stop and openly admit that to myself. What kind of person am I that I'm sitting here, praying that he's giving whoever shot up our house hell right now? That he's putting bullets into the heads of his enemies. No, not his enemies. Ours.

"Holly, you okay in there?" Helena knocks on the door.

"Yeah, I'll be out in a minute," I call back. I should go and deal with the ramifications of having Donatello's daughter turn up at my doorstep. I should warn her that Theo isn't in the frame of mind for a family reunion of any sorts at the moment.

So much for drinking my problems away today.

Chapter Seven

Well, that took longer than I expected. The old man had a lot of balls about him— that's for sure. Usually, breaking people down doesn't take me so long, but Beno wasn't just any random thug off the street. No, he was a Don—as he attempted to remind us over and over again at the end —and I just killed one of the five bosses of New York. (John Junior never officially took to the throne so, for all intents and purposes, that hit doesn't count.) Ask me if I regret the power move, and I'll tell you not one fucking bit. There are two more on my list. But they'll have to wait for another day.

"What are you going to do about this birthright shit?" Neo asks.

According to Beno, because I'm a Donatello by blood, I'm next in line for that throne. Like I want to take over another fucking family. I'm a Valentino; it's what I know. I have no desire or plans to move to fucking Italy and take over the fucking country. Donatello might have just killed off his underboss—at least that's the official story we've agreed upon, in order to maintain my wife's privacy and ensure her protection. But it's his problem to replace him, and it won't fucking be with me. Beno claims the other two wanted to eliminate me because of the power I'd wield over them, given my birthright. They're all fucking scared of the bastard.

They should direct that fear towards me, because I'm coming for each and every one of them. They set me up. They wanted me to insert myself in their sex trafficking scheme, knowing I'd be alone. Knowing I wouldn't say no to stopping that shit. They wanted to kill me off before Donatello could uncover my paternity. How the fuck they discovered the truth, I still haven't quite figured out. Maybe Holly is right. Maybe I do need to have a discussion with my mother.

"I'm not going to do fucking shit about it. What I'm

going to do is pick up my wife and take her the fuck home."

"Ah, yeah, about that. Holly's at her apartment. Helena called me earlier; she's with her."

"What the fuck is she doing there?"

"No idea, but Helena said to warn you. She's not in a good mood."

"No shit. I fucking left her in a café in a bathrobe to come save your ass."

"And I'm sure when you tell her as much, all will be forgiven. She loves me. She'll be glad you got there in the nick of time to keep my brains from being splattered all over the dining room." He grunts as my fist hits his arm. "Ow, what the fuck was that for?"

"My wife does not fucking love you, asshole," I groan.

"Yeah, she does. You know who else she loved? Sonnie, and she hasn't even had a chance to say goodbye to him."

"The funeral's planned for this coming Saturday. It took some time to arrange to have his body flown in."

"I know. But does she?"

I glare at my best friend. Why is he so concerned about my wife? I know I should be thankful, but fuck him. I don't bother answering his question. "Just drive me to her apartment."

I knock on the door. It's silent inside. Checking my watch, I see it's a little after eleven. Fuck, she's going to be pissed. I smile at the prospect of fucking the anger out of her.

"Maybe she's asleep. Don't you have a key."

"Do you think I'd be sitting out here if I had a fucking key?" I growl. I nod at the four men standing with their backs to the wall. "She still in there?" I ask them. I had them stationed in front of Helena's café before I even made it back to the house.

"Hasn't left," one of them says. I pivot, about to kick the fucking door in, when it swings open with an angry-looking Helena glaring at me with her arms folded.

"About fucking time," I growl.

I push past her and stop dead in my tracks. There, sitting on the couch, is Angelica fucking Donatello. Fuck me. I don't know how to process what I'm seeing right now. I've met her, years ago when we were kids. And I've seen photos of her in the tabloids. But looking at her now, it's sinking in that she's my fucking sister. Half sister. What the fuck is she doing here? I turn back to Helena. "Where's Holly?"

"Bedroom. But, Theo, you should know…"

I don't hear the rest of her sentence before I'm

quietly closing the bedroom door behind me. The bathroom light is on, blanketing the space with a soft glow. I walk and bend over the bed, stroking Holly's hair from her face. I gulp, preparing myself for the outburst she's likely to spew my way. Deservedly so too. I fucking left her, alone and barely dressed. Granted, I left her protected, but she doesn't know that. Was she scared?

"Dolcezza, wake up," I say softly, peppering light kisses on her pouty lips. Her eyes spring open, like she's been lying here awake. Waiting. Waiting for me, again. Even in the dim light, I can see the redness and swelling of her eyes. She's been crying, again. "Fuck, Holly, I'm sorry. So sorry."

She puts her fingers to her lips and looks behind her as she rises from the bed. That's when I notice she's not alone. What the fuck? There's a kid next to her. "Do not wake her up. Out now!" Holly whispers harshly.

I stand and stare down at the little girl asleep beneath the covers. Something in my heart twitches at the sight of her. Is it because the sight of Holly with a child is bloody appealing to me, or is it because I know the kid's my niece? Donatello's granddaughter. This is the little girl that, that fucking bastard Giovani was planning on stealing right out from under their noses. If anything, the weeks I spent in Italy weren't a total waste. At the very least, I'm thankful I got the information on that fucked-up plan and was able to put a stop to it. I let Holly shove me out of the bedroom door; she gently shuts it behind her.

"What the bloody hell, T? What right do you think you have to barge in here in the middle of the goddamn night?" she hisses as she makes her way to the kitchen.

"What right?" I raise my eyebrows and follow her. "You're my fucking wife. That's what right I have."

"Your wife? Really. Well, as your wife, I would have thought—gee, I don't know—knowing where you were all day would be a courtesy. Or how's this? Not leaving me in a bloody coffee shop, wearing nothing but a bathrobe."

"I told Helena to have you wait for me. I was coming back for you, dolcezza." I keep my voice calm—well, as calm as I can. I can't fucking help the fact that her anger turns me on. I pivot to glare at Helena. She had one fucking job.

"Don't look at her. This isn't her fault," Holly snaps. "And why didn't you two wake me up? That tequila had my name on it." She points to the coffee table, where two bottles of Patrón sit. One empty, one half-full.

"Well, you just looked so peaceful. And you didn't even make it through one story," Helena answers, while Angelica just stares between Holly and me.

Fuck this... There are too many people here. I need to get my wife alone. I'm not having this conversation in front of an audience. "Dolcezza, get your stuff. We're going home." I've been on the receiving end of a fuck-ton of icy death glares before. But none have ever rattled me as much as the one Holly is giving me now.

"And where exactly is home, T? In your penthouse, where two people were murdered and left to rot in our bed? At the brownstone that just got shot up this morning? Tell me, where is home, because I'm starting to lose track." She folds her arms over her chest, and my eyes are immediately drawn to her cleavage.

This is not how the night was supposed to go. I was planning on making her come so hard she forgot she was even mad at me to begin with. I can't do that with all these fucking people watching us. "Home is wherever you are, dolcezza. Home is wherever we are together. Tell me where you want to go, and I'll take you there." I wrap my arms around her rigid frame. It doesn't take long for her to relax and melt into me.

Then she remembers she's pissed and pushes me away. "No, you're not doing your voodoo shit on me right now. I'm not leaving this apartment tonight. So, either you can go home by yourself, or you can... I don't know what you can do, but I'm staying."

Bending forward, I pick her up and throw her over my shoulder, walking towards the balcony to get some semblance of privacy. "Neo, take Helena home," I tell him before I shut the sliding glass door behind us, ignoring the elephant in the room that is Angelica. I may not want to deal with her at the moment, but I'm not about to kick her or her daughter out in the middle of the night either. I don't know how to process the feelings I'm having for those two right now.

"Put me down, T. Bloody hell, it's freezing out here," Holly yells.

"Fuck. Sorry, dolcezza. Here, put this on." I take off

my jacket and wrap it around her shoulders. She accepts the gesture. And I don't miss the way she pulls the collar up and inhales deeply. I follow her to the ground as she sits with her back against the wall, staring out into the night sky.

"You left me... again," she says, breaking our silence.

"I know. I'm sorry, Holly. Fuck, I don't know what to do here."

"You promised you wouldn't leave me, and you just left me sitting in a coffee shop."

Lifting my thumb, I swipe at the silent tears falling down her cheeks. "I'm sorry. I had to, dolcezza. I had to go back, if I hadn't..." I let my sentence trail off.

"I know," she says, shocking me. "I know what you have to do, Theo. I just don't like it. I don't know if I can live like this. I'm not sure how much my heart can take, not knowing where you are all day and all night. Not knowing if you're safe. Not knowing if you're even still alive. I was scared. Not for myself, but for you."

"Dolcezza, I don't have a choice. We don't have a choice. This is my world. I'm not going to lie to you and tell you it's safe. Because you've seen for yourself how fucked up it really is. But this is it. The hand we've been dealt. We just have to find a way to make it work for us." I pick her up and pull her onto my lap, holding her gaze. "There is no other choice here, Holly. You're my wife. I'm never going to be able to let you go. Even if you were to beg, I couldn't. I can't. I need you. I fucking love you."

"The thought of leaving has never crossed my mind. It should have. Logically, I know that. But you are mine, T. I'm never going to ask you to let me go. I want you to hold on. I want to be what brings you home at night. I want to be your first choice. And as selfish as it is, I want to be your only choice as well. I don't like sharing you with your job."

Chapter Eight

Holly

I curl myself into T's arms. Taking comfort in his embrace, the warmth, the feeling of being safe. It's consuming me. It always does. How can one person have this effect on me? I try hard to remind myself that I'm pissed off at him. That I'm angry he left me sitting in a bloody café. I try not to let the relief of being in his arms take away from my anger. It's hard. So freaking hard. "We can't keep doing this, T. I can't keep doing this," I whisper into his chest.

He tilts my face up, making my eyes meet his. "I know, dolcezza. I know." He leans down and captures my lips with his. "I love you. You are more important to me than anything or anyone. I need you to know that. When I heard those shots this morning, my first thought was not running out and helping my men, protecting my family. It was you; it was getting you as far away from that house as quickly as I could. Once I knew you were safe at Helena's, I had to go back, Holly. You are my first thought, my every thought. But my family, the men who work for me. They rely on me too."

"I know. I understand. I just don't like it," I tell him honestly, sinking back into his chest. After sitting in silence for a few minutes, I bring up a subject that I know he's avoiding. "What are you going to do about Angelica? She's here to see you."

"I don't know what to do about that."

"It's not her fault, you know. You can't hate or blame her for what your mum did."

"Why are you always right? So wise."

"It's because I'm a teacher, and teachers know everything, obviously." I laugh.

"Come on, let's get you inside. It's fucking freezing out here," T says, lifting me to my feet.

I follow him back into the living room, which is now empty. "Where did everyone go?" I ask, just as Angelica is walking down the small hallway with Isabella in her arms.

"I'm sorry. I shouldn't have come here. It was lovely to meet you, Holly." Angelica heads for the door.

"Stop," T barks, using his gruff, commanding tone. Angelica pauses and raises an eyebrow, waiting for him to say something else. "Where are you planning on going?" he asks.

"I have a suite at the Four Seasons," she answers as Isabella wiggles her way out of her mother's arms.

"Are you my Uncle Theo?" the girl asks. The room is silent, both Angelica and I waiting on his answer just as much as his hopeful niece.

"Yes, you must be the little princess of Italy I've heard so much about." T bends down and holds his hand out for Isabella to shake. She looks at his open palm, then wraps her tiny arms around his neck, catching him off-guard. He slowly curls one hand around her back, patting her gently. It's a little comical and sweet. My damn ovaries are working overtime at the sight.

"I'm not really a princess, but my nonno thinks I am. I'm not going to tell him I'm not, because he buys me ponies," she says seriously.

"I think you could get anyone to buy you ponies, bella. All you'd have to do is ask."

"I think I have enough ponies now."

"Do you like ice cream? I was just about to take my girl home to get some. She's getting hangry," T not-so-subtly whispers. "Would you care to join us?"

Isabella looks to her mother for an answer. "Ah, we

should get back to the hotel, Izzy. I'm sure Theo and Holly have things they want to do."

"It's fine. There's plenty of space. I'll call ahead and have some rooms set up for you. Come on, bella, I don't know about you, but I could really use that ice cream." Theo takes hold of Isabella's hand. I'm left standing there, stunned and a little unsure of what to do.

Am I really jealous of an eight-year-old right now? No, I'm not. It's just that he'd usually be taking my hand. I don't have time to contemplate my uncertainty, before T reaches out and wraps his other arm around my shoulder, kissing my temple.

I melt into his side as he whispers, "Don't worry, dolcezza, you'll always be my number one girl." I glare up and elbow him in the ribs when I see the smirk he's sporting.

"We really can go back to the hotel, Theo. I didn't come here to impose on anyone," Angelica says, looking at the joined hands of Theo and Isabella as we walk out of the apartment.

"It's T, and you're not imposing. You're family. And there's a lot we have to catch up on. It would be easier to do that if you stay with us."

"Okay."

"Uncle T, I bet I can eat another three scoops quicker than you can," Isabella squeals over her bowl of midnight ice cream.

"You're on," T exclaims excitedly.

"Ah, no, you are not. It's time to get you back into bed, Izzy. Say thank you and goodnight."

"Grazie e buonanotte, Zio T e Zia Holly."

"Buonanotte, bella," T calls after the girl as Angelica shuffles her out of the kitchen.

Theo brought us to his family's estate. His mother isn't here, but I haven't asked him where she is. I plan on asking her myself tomorrow when we have our daily call. For the past half hour, I've watched T and Isabella talk and joke over a shared bowl of ice cream, like they've known each other their whole lives. It amazes me how they've managed to bond. I don't recall a time where I've seen T so relaxed—well, apart from when we're in bed, but that's a different kind of relaxed altogether.

"I think it's time I took you to bed too, dolcezza."

I'm honestly exhausted, and right now, all I want to do is curl up and go to sleep. "There is still a conversation we need to have, but it can wait until the morning. I'm tired, and I need sleep." My tone is sharper than I intended it to be. I guess I'm still harboring that anger from earlier after all.

"Okay, we'll talk tomorrow."

I shower quickly and jump into bed. I watch T as he strips off his shirt, and my mouth waters at the sight of him. Nope, I will not let my body betray my mind right now. I roll over and close my eyes, the events of the day playing on repeat. Ten minutes later, I feel him climb into the bed behind me, his strong arms caging me against his larger frame.

"Dolcezza, stop worrying. It will all work itself out. Ti voglio bene."

I roll over to face him. "I love you too. But you have to stop leaving me behind. We are either in this together, or we're not in this at all."

His eyes search mine silently for a few minutes, before he relents with a sigh. "We are in this together, always. I will work on not shutting you out of everything. But there will be times where I can't tell you things, for your own well-being. There will be times where I need to leave you behind, so I know you'll be safe. I won't apologize for trying to keep you safe, Holly."

"Okay." I lean into him and close my eyes. I feel his lips on the top of my head as sleep overtakes me.

The light streams through the curtains as I look around, trying to get my bearings and remember where I am. This waking up in different rooms is getting old. I think it's time that T and I find a place to live, somewhere we don't have to run away from. Somewhere that I can invite my family to visit and know they'll be safe from this world.

Carefully, I slip out from T's arm, hoping I don't wake him. Tiptoeing into the closet, I'm surprised to see a stack of new clothes, the shopping tags still attached. I really shouldn't be surprised... T always has whatever we need, wherever we end up.

I run my hands over the expensive fabrics, stopping at a black dress. There is no way Theo actually chose any of these. But I'm thankful to whoever did. I tear the label off and pull the material up my body. It's a Dolce and Gabbana fitted bodycon dress. It ends just above my knees at a respectable level, but shows all of my curves, and the cleavage boost is next-level. I grab a pair of patent leather pumps and shuffle into the bathroom. Shutting the door, I do my hair and makeup.

As I stare into my reflection, I finally emit a sense of strength that's been missing the past few weeks. It feels good to look good. I've been sitting around in yoga pants and Theo's shirts for way too long. I take one last peek in the mirror. "It's time to start acting like the queen everyone is claiming you are, Holly," I whisper to myself and walk back through the bedroom.

T is still asleep. I'm not surprised he hasn't stirred. He hasn't been sleeping lately. And I'm not about to wake him either. I have plans today, and I need to get out of this house before he notices. I make it down to the kitchen without running into anyone. However, that's where my luck runs out. "Fuck! Holly, what on...

what are you wearing?" Neo sputters the coffee he was drinking.

I look down at myself. "A dress?" I question, my brows drawn down in confusion.

He shakes his head. "That's not a dress, babe. That's a fucking death sentence."

"It's just a dress, Neo. How on earth can a dress be a death sentence?" I fill a cup of coffee from the pot he must have just made.

"Anyone caught looking at you in that is bound to meet the bottom of a shallow grave. I can't believe T even let you out of the room like that." He smirks.

I tilt my head. "You're looking at me in this dress. And T's still asleep."

That drops the smirk right off his face. "For the love of God, go and change, Holly."

I raise an eyebrow at him, while gulping down the hot liquid gold that is caffeine. Placing the cup in the sink, I ignore Neo as I search through the kitchen drawer—the same drawer I've seen T drop keys into before. I don't even care whose car they belong to at this point. I just need a way to get around. I inspect the first set I pick up and smile at the Ferrari logo staring back at me.

"Wait, what in the ever-loving fuck are you doing?" Neo asks, jumping to his feet and shuffling around the counter.

"I'm running some errands," I say, turning and walking in what I can only hope is the direction of the garage.

"No, you're not. You can't leave this house alone, Holly. Go and wake up your husband. I'm sure he'll take you anywhere you need to go." Neo follows me.

"Or... here's a thought: you could come with me if you're so concerned. I'm not waking Theo up. He needs to sleep."

"Cazzo, per favore non lasciarmi morire per questo," Neo mumbles in Italian.

I push open a door, thankful I somehow managed to remember where the garage was. When I step forward though, my mouth drops. During Theo's initial tour of this house, he simply pointed at the door and said: that's just the garage. He forgot to mention what was inside. This isn't your regular house garage; it's a bloody museum of cars. Fast cars. All lined up like a little kid would line up their collection of Match-boxes. I click the button on the keys in my hand and point, waiting to see which option lights up or makes a noise. My smile widens when I spot the shiny red convertible. Yes! This, this is exactly what I need today.

"Where are you planning on going anyway?" Neo asks as he snatches the keys out of my hands.

"Ah, no. That's not how this is going today. Give them back." I hold out my palm.

"Not a fucking chance in hell, babe. I am not getting in a car with you behind the wheel." He laughs as he makes the sign of the cross over his body.

My hands go to my hips. "Fine, I'll just take a different car. It's not like there aren't enough choices here."

"No, you're not. Get in and stop acting petulant." Neo opens the passenger's side door.

Did that asshole really just call me petulant? I smile, even though my blood is boiling. I'm sure he can see the redness I can already feel creeping up my neck. "Hold that thought," I say, pulling my phone out of my handbag. I need to know where I'm actually going. I call Gloria. She will know what to do.

"Holly, how are you? How's Theo?" she rushes out.

"Ah, fine. He's good, Gloria. I need a favor."

"Sure, anything. What do you need?"

"I need an appointment with a realtor. I'm going house shopping." I smirk at the shock that crosses Neo's face.

"Oh, yes, of course. Give me five minutes, and I'll text you the name of the only realtor I trust. I'll tell him to expect your call."

"Thank you." I hang up, and without taking my eyes off Neo, I place the phone back into my bag and swap it for the small handgun T gave me a while ago. My grip is unusually steady as I raise and point the barrel at Neo. I'm not really prepared to shoot him. At least, I don't think I am. "Give me the bloody keys, now."

"Put that down before you hurt someone, or your-self, sweetheart." He smiles like a lunatic.

"The only person who will get hurt here is you. I've shot you once before, Neo. Don't think I won't do it again. Only this time, you won't be wearing a bloody bulletproof vest."

"T is going to kill me for this, so what the hell? Why not go out with a goddamn bang? Here you are, your highness. I guess you're driving?" he concedes, handing the keys over.

Huh, this whole queen thing might just be what I needed after all.

Fifteen minutes into the drive, my phone rings. I look down at it and choose to ignore the call. The ringing stops and starts again right away. I know it's wrong, but I'm going to let him sweat for a little—see how much he likes it when he doesn't know where his person is. Because he's my person. The one I don't ever want to experience another day without again.

Neo looks at my phone. "You should answer that, you know. I don't think the world will ever be ready for a Theo Valentino who can't locate his wife."

The phone rings again, and I press decline. "I know." Neo's phone starts ringing next. He pulls it out of his pocket. "Don't answer it," I tell him.

"You might get away with not answering his calls, but I can guarantee you that I won't." He unlocks the screen and lifts the receiver to his ear.

Chapter Nine

I wake up, rolling over to reach out for Holly, except all I find is emptiness and cold bedsheets. I jump up, suddenly alert. "Holly, dolcezza," I call out. She's probably just in the bathroom. I get nothing but silence in return. My heart quickens as I rush out of bed and into the bathroom. She's not in there, but she has been. There's a ton of makeup and hair products left behind on the counter.

I relax a little. She must be downstairs. I get

dressed and rapidly descend the staircase in search of my wife. She's safe. Nothing can touch her in this house. That's what I'm telling myself anyway. I search the kitchen, living room, and dining room. A cold sweat breaks out when I can't find her.

"Holly!" I yell, waiting to hear her call back. Nothing. Fuck!

One of the guards comes into the dining room, cautiously approaching me. "Boss, Mrs. Valentino left about fifteen minutes ago."

Someone is about to fucking die. "You let her fucking leave the house? Alone? What the fuck do I pay you all for?" I hiss.

"No, she was with Neo, boss," he says before walking out the door, aware that if he were to stay any longer, his life would be on the fucking line. She's with Neo. Well, at least she isn't fucking alone, but where the fuck is she? What the fuck are they doing? And why didn't either of them wake me up?

I dial her number and the call goes straight to voicemail. "Sorry I missed your call..." I hang up and redial. And again, the call goes to voicemail.

"Answer your fucking phone," I scream into the empty room. I dial Neo; he answers after almost letting it ring out. That fucker knows better than to ignore my fucking calls, especially when he's taken off somewhere with my fucking wife. "Where the fuck are you?"

"Well, good morning to you too, boss. You slept well, I see."

"Don't fuck with me, Neo. Where the fuck is my

wife? And why'd I have to hear it from a fucking foot soldier that you've taken her out somewhere?"

"First off, don't get your panties all twisted. She's fine. She's here, in the car, right next to me. And I didn't take her anywhere. She took me. By gunpoint, I might add."

I understand his words, but they aren't making sense. *By gunpoint?* "You really expect me to believe that my wife pulled a gun on you, forced you to get into a car and drove off? To go where, exactly?"

"Well, I was taken by surprise too. It seems our girl is all grown up and taking hostages."

"*My* girl, Neo. She's my fucking girl. Not *ours*, certainly not yours, and sure as fuck not anyone else's. She's fucking mine. Where. The. Fuck. Is. She?" I yell.

"Okay, clearly, your parents should have had more children. You're starting to sound like a spoiled only child. I haven't stolen your favorite toy, T. I was forced to go along. Either that, or she was going alone."

"Where is she, Neo?" My voice is calm. I'm really ready to kill my best friend right now.

"Fanculo, hold on. I'll put you on speaker. Okay, she's here."

"Dolcezza, are you okay?" I ask.

"Morning. I'm fine. How are you?" Am I being punked? Does she not realize I'm losing my mind over here?

"I'd be fucking a hell of a lot better if I didn't wake up to an empty bed, not knowing where the fuck my wife was," I grunt.

"Okay, well, obviously I'm fine and you just need to chill out a bit, T. I'm running errands. I'll be back whenever I get back."

"Yeah, that's not how this is going to work, dolcezza. Where are you? I'll come and meet you."

"I'm shopping. You don't have to come meet me. I'm fine. Just do whatever it is you do all day. And talk to Angelica." The line cuts out before I can contemplate a reply. She hung up on me. What the fuck? I fire off a message to Neo.

Me: I want an address as soon as she stops somewhere.

Neo: Sure thing, boss. But if she asks, you didn't hear this from me. I suggest you speak to your mother's realtor. That's who she's meeting.

A realtor? What the fuck does Holly want with a realtor? Does she think she's moving out? Then again, moving out of where, exactly? Ever since we've been married, I've done nothing but move her from one place to the other. What I should have done was buy a fucking house, somewhere we could finally start our life together. Given some semblance of stability, instead of the shitshow that's been the entirety of our marriage. I'm about to head out to the garage when Angelica comes to a stop in front of me.

We stare at each other in silence. She really is a beautiful girl. I have no idea what to say to her. I don't know how to be a fucking brother. I've never had to be one, and now I have to be a brother to a... sister? Donatello couldn't have had another fucking son?

"This is weird, isn't it?" Angelica breaks the silence.

"To say the least. Did you sleep well? Do you need anything? Isabella okay?" I ask. That little girl managed to steal my heart within a matter of seconds. A heart I wasn't even sure existed before I met Holly.

"Yes, fine. She's still asleep. I don't usually let her stay up so late."

"Good." The awkward silence fills the room again.

"Come, you look like you could use a coffee."

I follow Angelica to the kitchen, when really, all I want to do is get in the car and hunt down my fucking wife. The Italian princess goes about making a fresh pot of coffee. I watch as she opens and shuts cupboards until she finds everything she needs.

"I didn't come here to cause trouble for you, Theo," she says.

"Then why *did* you come?" I ask, watching her move around. She may be my sister, but I'm not stupid. This girl was raised by the Don of all Dons. A ruthless motherfucker. Anyone foolish enough to deem her harmless deserves whatever's coming to them.

"I came to thank you. Papa told me what you did. That you heard what they were planning for my Izzy."

"You don't need to thank me for that, Angelica. I would have done the same for anyone," I grunt out, my rage simmering beneath the surface, imagining what could have happened to the little girl.

"She's all I have, Theo. So, I am thanking you, because if anything had happened to her, I don't know that I could survive that."

"How old are you anyway?" I wondered this last night. Did Donatello already have a family before he and my mother did whatever it was they did?

"Twenty-five. Why?"

Well, at least she's four years younger than me. It does feel a little better to know my mother wasn't involved with a married man with children. Although, for all I know, Donatello could have been married to Angelica's mother. I run the math over in my head. Isabella said she was eight. If Angelica is twenty-five, she would have had to have been seventeen when she had the girl. Who the fuck knocked her up when she was so young?

"Who's Isabella's father?" I ask, not sure that it's any of my business, but I'm going to make it so.

Angelica looks taken aback by my question. "It doesn't matter. He's not around."

"It does matter. Why isn't he around?" I'm getting more and more pissed off that she was left to raise a child on her own, when she was a fucking child herself.

"What do you think happened to the guy who impregnated Al Donatello's sixteen-year-old daughter, Theo?"

"I'd like to think he ended up with a fucking bullet between his eyes," I grunt.

"Exactly. Which is why he's no longer in the picture."

I look into her eyes. I can't tell if she's sad about his absence, or relieved. "Were you in love with him?" I ask, though I'm not convinced a sixteen-year-old could really be in love in the first place. I'm nearly thirty and I've only just discovered what it feels like.

"I was in love with the idea of him. Not necessarily the man himself. He made me feel special. Like I wasn't just an object to use for my connections. I wanted to matter to someone. He didn't know who I was. I lied and gave him a fake name. I only knew him for three months."

"You do matter to people, Angelica," I say, wanting to offer her whatever comfort I can. I stand. "I've got to go and meet my wife. But stay. Make yourself at home."

Walking down the hall, I find Lucas, one of the guards. "That girl is my sister. She's off-limits to everyone. Spread the word. Also, get five men ready to follow me."

"Sure, boss," he answers, without questioning me further, then speaks into the mic piece in his ear. I head to the garage and smile as I note the only empty parking spot. Of course, Holly took that one.

My old man was a car enthusiast; it seems my wife is too.

Chapter Ten

Holly

I pull up the tree-lined driveway of the address the agent texted me. He said he would meet us here. I'm stunned by the picturesque scenery. I thought T's parent's house was impressive. I mean, it is impressive, but this... this is something else altogether. It's taken about forty-five minutes to get out here from the city. I wonder if that's too far away for Theo? The private entrance circles around a huge water feature. I stop behind a car that's parked near the stairs.

"Damn, Hol, this is one hell of a house," Neo mumbles as he exits from the passenger side.

"It's too much, isn't it? Do you think it's too far? It seems quiet out here," I observe as I look around the perfectly manicured grounds.

"Because it is fucking quiet. This is the definition of suburbia." He shudders, like the idea of living in a family neighborhood creeps him out.

"Well, it's a good thing you don't have to live here," I sass.

"Are you kidding? With all the bored MILFs out here, you won't be able to get rid of me. Oh! We can do lunch at the country club and all."

"Hard pass. Come on, let's look inside." The door opens as I'm halfway up the stairs, and a wiry blond man stands there with a polite smile as he assesses me. Do I look like I can't afford this house? Wait, *can* I afford this house? I have no idea how much a place like this even costs. Judging from the lease on my tiny apartment, I can only assume that this house is way out of my league. But I'm not about to let this real estate agent best me. I straighten my shoulders and continue up the stairs with Neo right behind me.

"Holly? Hi, I'm Mark."

"Mrs. Valentino," I correct. "It's a pleasure to meet you." I hold out my hand. Neo chuckles into a cough behind me, and I throw a slight elbow back at him.

"Right, Mrs. Valentino. Come in, let me show you around. As you can see, no expense has been spared on this property. There're seventeen bedrooms, eighteen bathrooms, a guest house, and a pool house behind the main house."

What does anyone need that many rooms for? I crane my neck to survey the massive open foyer. There's a staircase on each side, which meet at a balcony at the top. The floors are white and black marble. There's so much opulence... and we've only just entered the house. I don't know what Gloria told this guy, but I think he may have the wrong idea when it comes to what Theo and I actually need.

"Through here is a state-of-the-art kitchen: all European appliances, stone countertops..."

I don't listen to whatever else he rambles on about. I'm stunned by the beauty that is this kitchen. The windows overlook the gardens and a huge resort-style swimming pool. As I stare outside, I can picture kids running around, swimming, having fun. To my left, there's an eat-in dining area that would be perfect for family meals.

As we walk through the rest of the lower floor, which seems never-ending, I get more and more attached to the idea of raising a family with Theo. Is this house too much? Absolutely, but I'd be lying if I said it wasn't my dream come true. There's a library—a huge freaking library. A game room, two offices, three living rooms, and a formal dining room with enough space for at least forty people.

"Take your time on the upper floors. I'll be down here if you have any questions," Mark says.

"Thank you." I wait until we're upstairs and out of

earshot before I speak. "This house is insane. It's obviously way too much. But still, a girl can dream, right?" I laugh.

"Why is it too much?" Neo questions. When I turn to look at him, he's staring at me with genuine confusion.

"Ah, because a house like this must cost a few million, right?"

Neo laughs, like full-on belly laughs. "You're cute," he says. He pulls his phone out of his pocket and walks in the opposite direction, firing off a text message.

I navigate the winding halls. A scream escapes me as I'm grabbed from behind, and a hand covers my mouth. I attempt to throw my elbows back, stomp my foot, all the things my brother-in-law once tried to teach me. But none of it works. And then I smell him. Theo. I bite down on his hand. Hard. "Ow, fuck! Dolcezza, calm down. It's me," he hisses, shaking his arm out and turning me around.

"I know," I growl at him.

"Then why the fuck did you bite me?"

"Because you scared the shit out of me, T."

"I scared you? Well, how do you think I felt waking up to a cold fucking bed this morning with my wife gone?"

"Not nearly as bad as I felt watching a building blow up, thinking my husband was inside?" I throw back at him. "How do you think I felt when I thought you were freaking dead for three days?"

He looks stricken with guilt. Good, he should be.

"I'm sorry. Dolcezza, I'm sorry. But you can't just leave the house like that, not telling me, not taking any security with you. It's not safe. There are dangerous men in my world, Holly."

My blood boils. I can feel my hands physically shaking as I recall just how dangerous the men in his world are. "Don't you think I know that? Don't you think I've experienced that enough?" I yell at him, tears streaming down my face as I swipe angrily at them.

"Fuck, Holly. I'm sorry. Of course you know. I'm sorry," he says again, wrapping his arms around me.

"You know you're saying that a lot lately. I don't need you to be sorry, Theo. I need you to stop fucking up. You are my rock, my foundation, and lately that foundation feels like it's cracking."

"I will be whatever you need me to be. I will do whatever you need me to do. I've never had to do this before, dolcezza. Am I likely to fuck up again? Yes. But I promise you are my priority. You *are* my number one. I just... I don't know what the fuck I'm doing."

"I need you to be my husband. That's all. I need you to be the guy I fell for, within a matter of hours. I need you to be that man. That's all."

He smirks down at me. "A matter of hours, huh? Well, shit, Holly, you had me in *seconds*."

I smile. "Hallmark line." That's the Theo I fell in love with, the one who would deliver cheesy lines at the drop of a hat, the one who seemed like he had everything under control and nothing could penetrate his cool. I feel a little guilty expecting him to be that, considering what he's been through lately. No one could lose a parent, take over the family business (especially his kind of family business), find out your dad isn't your biological father, and remain unaffected. "I'm sorry, I shouldn't have said that. I just need... I don't know what I need."

T looks around the bedroom we're in. "Well, it appears you need a house, and that's something I can actually give you."

"I want a *home*, not a house, T. I want somewhere we can start a family, somewhere we'll be safe, somewhere that's sacred to just us."

"Okay, well, what do you think of this one?"

"I love this house, but it's too much. And it's a long way from the city."

"I'm not sure if you noticed, but we have cars, dolcezza, plenty of them. The distance to the city is nothing but a drive. If you like this house, consider it yours."

"Ours," I correct him.

"Ours... I like that. Let's go talk to the realtor." He takes my hand in his and leads me back downstairs.

I didn't even get to explore all that the upper levels have to offer, but I don't need to. This house is freaking amazing. When we get back to the main living area, Mark is sitting on a sofa, looking rather uncomfortable with five of Theo's soldiers standing around the edges of the room.

T walks in and nods his head once, and all five men exit at the same time. We sit on the sofa opposite the realtor. "Mark, it seems my wife is fond of this house. What's the asking price?" Theo says in what I've come to learn is his *all-business* voice.

"Forty-million, Mr. Valentino."

I almost choke on air. I cough into my hand and look at my husband, who somehow appears unfazed. "Call the owners. If they can be out and settle within seven days, I'll give them thirty-five—*cash*."

My eyes widen at him. Is he serious right now? "Ah, T? I think we should talk about this," I whisper.

He looks at me and smirks, then returns his glare to Mark. "What are you waiting for? Call them," he barks. "I'm a busy man, Mark. I have plenty of other things I need to get done today."

"Ah, yes, of course, Mr. Valentino." The man stands and walks out of the room with his phone to his ear.

"I trust that you're aware it's in the best interest of your health to get this deal secured within the next ten minutes," T calls out. The realtor pales as he nods silently.

I slap Theo on the shoulder. "You cannot threaten the real estate agent, T. That poor man is scared shitless."

"I can, and I did. And he should be scared. You want this house, Holly, and I'm going to make sure you get it."

The intentions are good. The actions, however? Not so much. "T, I want the house, but I don't want it if the only way we can get it is to threaten people. Also, thirty-five million dollars, who the hell has that kind of money sitting around? That's insane. Do you know how many starving kids that money could feed? Oh my God, am I a bad person for wanting this house, when so many people don't even have a place to live?"

T picks me up and sits me on his lap. "Dolcezza, breathe. It's going to be okay. The fact that you think about those less fortunate makes you one of the best kinds of people. And to answer your question, we do. We have that kind of cash."

"Okay, but are you sure it's not too far? Will this place be secure enough?" I worry my bottom lip.

He leans in and kisses me. "I'll make sure it's secure enough. And if this is where you want to build our lives, then so do I."

"I love you, T, warts and all," I say, kissing him back deeper.

"I love you more and more every day. Just when I think I can't possibly love you more than I already do, I wake up and feel an even stronger connection to you."

"Hallmark moment," I whisper as I hike up my tight dress so I can straddle him. I grind against his hardened cock.

"Fuck, Holly, you know I missed my breakfast this morning, and I'm fucking starving."

"Uh-huh, maybe you should do something about that," I groan, my panties getting wetter and wetter. And then, T is lifting me up and readjusting my dress so it falls back down to my knees. I'm confused and dazed by his sudden actions... by the rejection.

As I stand there, wondering for the second time if my husband doesn't want me anymore, Mark enters the room. T smirks and tugs me on the sofa next to him.

How the hell did he know he'd walk back in at that very second? Does my husband have Spidey senses?

Chapter Eleven

"**Y**ou're moving to the fucking suburbs, T? You might as well just give up your balls now." Neo laughs from the passenger seat.

I had the documents for the house within an hour of heading towards the city. I dropped Holly back off at my parents' estate—made sure every fucking soldier knew that she wasn't to leave the house alone. And if she does leave, they're instructed to call me before the tires even hit the driveway. I'm hoping she'll be too busy with Angelica and Isabella to need to go anywhere anyway. I double-park in front of the liquor store Holly made me promise I'd stop at. Apparently, she *borrowed*—her words—two bottles of tequila yesterday that she didn't even get to drink.

"I'll be right back," I tell Neo as he curses at the car honking its fucking horn behind me. The racket stops as soon as I step out of the car and stare through the fucker's window. Ignoring the impatient son of a bitch, I jog into the shop and throw a couple of hundreds on the counter. The young kid behind the register just stares at them. "My wife said she owed you some money. The Valentinos always repay their debts. Have a nice day."

I walk out and jump back into the car. Neo shakes his head at me. "So, the suburbs? Are we getting house staff? Because an estate that big is going to need maids, lots of them, in those hot little uniforms too. I'll even do the hiring for you."

"Yeah, sure. Run that one by my wife." I laugh.

"Why do you have to suck all the fun out of things? You know what? I bet I can talk her around. She's not going to be able to keep up a house like that by herself."

I give him a side eye roll. "You know, I wouldn't put it past her to castrate you if you even mention bringing half-naked women in flimsy maid uniforms into her house."

"Yeah, maybe. But to do that, she'd have to touch my dick. And I know for a fact you wouldn't let that happen, so I think I'm safe."

"Fottuto idiota!" I curse him out. He's right though. There's no fucking way I'd let her touch his dick.

"What are we doing anyway?" Neo asks.

"We're going to work," I say, pulling into the Valentino Empire building. I have many offices across the city, but this is home base. It's also the one my father frequented.

"Right, and why are we going to work when there's a fucking war raging in your city?"

"*Because* we need to make money. The shit doesn't print itself. Besides, we have to get back to a normal routine. Holly wants things to settle down. We have to put a fucking end to this war and move on with our lives."

"Right, because Holly wants you to."

"What's with the attitude? If you have something to say, just fucking say it."

"Nope, nothing." He gets out, slamming the door. Anyone else, I would have shot already.

"What's your problem with Holly? I thought you liked her."

"I do like her. That being said, I don't know if you've noticed, but she's changing, man. She's turning into someone different. This world, it's changing her. And I don't know if it's for the better."

"What I see is my wife getting stronger. Something she needs to do... if she's going to survive in this family. I see her standing her ground more often. Not being frightened of her own fucking shadow. Yeah, she's changing but in the best possible way."

"You don't think it's weird that she killed that fucker and hasn't even lost a wink of sleep? Do you remember your first kill? Because I sure as fuck do."

"She hasn't processed it yet. I know that. But when she does, if she needs to fall, we'll be there to pick her back up."

"You know that girl loves you to the ends of the earth. The things she'll do for you... well, it's fucking scary. Don't break her, T."

"Not that it's any of your business, but I don't plan on fucking breaking her."

"Really? It wasn't any of my business when I had to pick her up off the floor when she contemplated following you to the grave, because the thought of a life without you was too much for her. But yeah, sure, it's none of my fucking business."

I watch Neo storm off into the building. He barges through the door that leads to the stairs. Fucking idiot. I nod politely at everyone as I make my way to the bank of elevators.

"Good morning, Mr. Valentino. How are you, sir? Can I get you anything? Coffee? Tea?"

I'm trying to figure out who the hell this chick is, but I come up blank. "Who the fuck are you?" I ask her.

"Ah, I'm Brittany, sir. I was appointed your secretary. I guess the other girl quit, so now I'm all yours." She flutters her eyelashes. *Yeah, that's not going to happen.*

I turn and walk into my office, slamming the door behind me. This space gives me an odd sense of peace, the view of Central Park somewhat relaxing. I sit down and fire up my computer. I've done as much as I could for our legitimate companies while I've been away. But, it's not the same as actually being here. Opening my emails, I can see I haven't done as well at keeping up as I thought. I buzz through to Brittany and tell her to hold my calls for the morning. I need to focus on this shit.

The door swings open. I have my hand on the gun strapped to the underside of my desk and I'm just about ready to draw, when I see Holly walk through.

"I'm sorry, sir. She wouldn't wait." Brittany gives my wife the evil eye and pushes her way forward.

"That's because I don't have to wait." Holly smiles sweetly. "Isn't that right, babe?"

"That's right." I smile. I really fucking love the new Holly with all her sass; it's a fucking turn on.

"Uncle T, Auntie Holly said you can see the whole

world from your office." Isabella runs straight up to me, throwing her little arms around my neck.

"Well, I don't know about the whole world, but you get a good glimpse of the city." I turn her around to face the window.

"We're up really high. Aren't you scared you're going to fall?" Isabella questions.

I laugh. "No, *bella*, I'm not scared of falling. Where's your mom?" I ask the kid, but look to Holly for an answer.

"Oh, Neo wanted to chat with her. She's in his office. We brought you lunch." Holly holds up a brown paper bag. Whatever is in it smells fucking amazing. Just then my stomach growls, and I look at my watch to see I've been sitting here, behind this computer, for hours without stopping.

Holly's words sink in, and within seconds, I'm out of my seat. *She's in his office.* My sister's in Neo's office... No fucking way is he getting his grubby fucking hands on her. I know exactly what my cousin does with the women in his office. "I'll be right back, dolcezza. Why don't you two set up on the conference table over there?" I point to the seating area off to the side of the room.

"Ah, sure. Come on, Izzy, you can help."

I storm out the door, and fucking Brittany follows me. "Mr. Valentino, is there anything I can get you?"

"No, but don't ever try to stop my wife from entering my office again. You won't like the consequences if you do." I throw open the door to Neo's office.

He's leaning against his desk. Angelica is sitting in the chair in front of him. He looks at his watch. "Two minutes. You owe me a hundred." He extends a hand to Angelica, who grunts as she pulls out a hundred-dollar bill from her bag and slams it into Neo's open palm.

"What the fuck are you doing?" I ask. "And *this*— yeah, not fucking happening. I will fucking shoot you first." I point between them, but direct the threat to Neo.

Angelica stands and places her hands on her hips. "No, you don't get to roll in on your high horse and try to scare guys away. If I want to screw his brains out, guess what? I will. If I want to sleep my way through all of your men, I will. My body is mine to do with as I please. Not yours, or anyone else's."

"You're right. *You* can do whatever you want, Angelica." I nod my head at her. "But so can I. And if I want to put a bullet between the eyes of each and every man who's stupid enough to touch you, if I have to kill every last one of them, that's my fucking choice."

"Oh my God, you're worse than Papa. I don't even know you. And you don't know me. Why do you care who I'm sleeping with?" Her arms fold under her chest. I don't miss how Neo's fucking eyes are drawn straight to her cleavage.

"No!" I point to him again. "I don't need to know

you. You're my sister, Angelica. Family is everything to me. You're now a part of that."

I see her resolve slowly dissipate. "I wish you were a sister. I would have liked a sister better. Thank God you came with Holly."

"She's the best part of me." I shrug. "Come on, she's waiting for us."

Holly left with Angelica and Isabella not long after we finished lunch. But not before Angelica dropped the bomb that her father was in town. My biological father. What the fuck is Al Donatello doing in New York? He has rarely stepped a foot out of Italy in all the years I've been old enough to know who the fuck he is.

I'm back behind my desk, going over reports and trying to focus on business, while my mind is set on trying to figure out how to put an end to this fucking mafia war bullshit. I've always loved my dark underworld, loved the lifestyle, the job, the money, the cars, the women. But now, being at the head of it all, trying to keep the whole fucking family in check... it's fucking draining. It's just one fucking issue after another. Staring out the window, I wonder what it would be like to leave it all behind. Get new identities and find a fucking deserted island somewhere. I couldn't do that to Holly though. I couldn't tear her away from her family. I run a hand over my face. Turning back to the computer, I attempt to skim the report on the screen. The sound of my phone shrills through the silent room.

"Valentino."

"T? I don't have long, but you need to listen to me."

I straighten in my chair. "L? Where the fuck are you, and where've you been? Neo said he hasn't heard from you since you left Italy."

"I know. I've been on the DL. I'm fine. I'm staying with Alexei. But listen... I heard something. From my uncle. He said something about the Clover being in bed with Hal and Leo. He said they've put a hit out on you." I laugh in response. I can't help it. "It's not funny, T. I'm serious," Lana hisses through the receiver.

"I know, L. Look, I'm fine. Neo's fine. We'll be fine. Let the fuckers try to come for me. I can't fucking wait. Where are you anyway? Are you safe?"

"Are you worried about me, T?" she questions.

"Not at all. You're like a cat. You have many fucking lives."

"Thanks. I'm fine. I'm just laying low with Alexei. Can you believe I'm getting married?"

"You really think your families are going to let this happen? You running off and marrying a fucking Russian?"

"Well, it's happening, and I honestly don't think they care too much anymore. Dad's gone. My brother's gone. I'm not of any concern to anyone."

"You're wrong. Neo happens to care about you a lot," I tell her.

"Yeah, just Neo? Look, I've gotta go, but give Holly my best, and tell Neo to stop worrying."

"Yeah, okay. Be smart, L. Don't do anything without first considering the consequences. Again." I hang up the phone and shut down my computer. I need to get out of this fucking office. I need to get home to my wife. Tomorrow is Sonnie's funeral, and I know it'll be a hard day for her. It could just be the thing to send her spiraling. Neo was right. It's not normal to be so... *okay* with everything that happened in Italy.

You don't get assaulted and almost raped, shoot and kill your attacker, and walk away without a backwards glance. She's been acting like everything is fine, like *she* is fine. I wonder if it's just that. *An act.* Surely, I'd be able to tell if she wasn't all right. I know her. I know her fucking soul. I would be able to tell if anything was bothering her. Well, more than my usual fuckups anyway.

Chapter Twelve

Holly

I'm bored out of my mind. It's been six hours and twenty-two minutes since I left T's office after lunch. But it's not like I'm counting or anything. I don't know what to do with myself. I've video chatted with my mum and dad, with Reilly and Bray, and with Alyssa, who just gave birth to a beautiful little baby boy. They named him Ash. I love him already. I wish I was there to cuddle up with him. I went online and sent them one of almost everything blue I could find in the baby store.

I'm pacing the shelves of my in-laws' huge library. There's nothing here I want to read though, and I don't know where my kindle is. I need something to escape my own mind, something to escape this boredom. What I really need is to go back to work. I need a purpose other than being Mrs. Valentino. I move over to the desk and open the MacBook that's on the table. I have no idea whose computer it is, but I'm hoping that it's not password protected and already connected to the internet.

I laugh when I open it and the blank password box stares back at me. Of course it wouldn't be that easy. These men are paranoid as shit. Theo has two passwords on his phone alone. Don't ask me how that works because I have no idea. But if you do get through the first one, you then have to get past the second before you can access anything in the device.

"Something amusing?" a gravelly voice asks, making me jump like I've just been caught with my hand in the cookie jar.

"Jesus, T, you have to stop scaring me like that. I'm too young to have a heart attack," I scold him while eye-fucking him. *Hard.* He's leaning against the doorframe, his hands in his pockets, with the sleeves of his white business shirt rolled up to his elbows and his tie undone around his neck. Damn, he makes one fine picture. My mouth waters at the sight.

He growls as he steps forward, kicking the door shut. "If you keep looking at me like that, dolcezza, I'm the one at risk of having a heart attack."

"How am I looking at you?" I ask, watching him slowly make his way over to the desk.

"Like you're hungry, and I'm your next meal."

"Well, perhaps I am. But I don't see how that would give you a heart attack."

He reaches the desk, spins the chair around, and drops to his knees in front of me. Grabbing my chin between his fingers, he says, "I'm going to fuck you hard and fast until everyone in this fucking house can hear you scream my name. And then I'm going to do it all over again. And again. And again."

"Oh, okay." What do I say to that? Maybe a *yes please*? My other thought is: *why haven't you started yet?* But I don't get a chance to say anything before T is running his fingers up and down my calves.

He reaches the hem of my skirt. "I don't like this dress," he mumbles.

"What's wrong with the dress?"

"You look too fucking hot in it. Do you have any idea how hard I was at lunch, being able to look but not touch, because you didn't come alone?"

"Mmm, how hard?"

"Fucking *rock* hard. I had to go into the bathroom after you left and relieve myself."

"Well, you could have asked me to stay. It's not like I had anything else to do."

"We will come back to that statement later. But

right now, I need a taste." He pushes my dress up past my hips, pulling my ass to the edge of the seat. His fingers tug my panties to the side, and his tongue runs along the length of my pussy, bottom to top. One long, slow lick.

My fingers go straight to his hair. "Mmm, I missed you today."

"I miss you every second I'm not touching you, dolcezza," he says before leaning in and licking again. The vibration from the growl that leaves his lips runs through my core.

"Oh God! Shit, T!" I was so worked up just from looking at him; it's not going to take much to push me over the edge.

"Louder! I want to hear your screams echo off the fucking walls, Holly." Well, if he keeps doing that thing with his tongue the whole of New York will hear me. His tongue pushes into my pussy, in and out, in and out, before he runs it back up to my clit. It's like he has a map, or his tongue has a magnetic connection with my clit because the man never freaking misses.

His teeth graze over my hardened, sensitive bud. "Oh God!" I grind up, lifting my hips to meet his mouth, my hands now clinging to the armrests of the chair. My nails are probably ruining the leather. Not that I care. All I care about is chasing this high to the end.

T's fingers tease my opening, before they dip in and then out. He drags a finger around and circles my back hole. Oh shit, I squirm. I know I freaking like it when he does this to me, but it still feels so dirty. So forbidden. So... *everything*. The moment he pushes forward, my whole body tenses up, the sensations running through every nerve ending. "Relax, dolcezza, you're going to rip my finger right off." T laughs.

"Oh God!" My palms cover my face in embarrassment. Shit, I will myself to relax.

T uses his free hand to pull my arms down. He looks me directly in the eye. "Good girl. Just relax and let me make you feel good."

Something is very wrong with my psyche, because the moment he praises my response, my pussy gushes. T smirks up at me before his tongue dips in, and he sucks. He literally sucks like he's drinking his beverage of choice. My thighs quake. I'm a squirming, writhing mess. His tongue travels up to my clit and circles before his mouth closes over and his teeth nibble. His finger in my back hole starts moving slowly. My head falls against the chair as I give in to the pleasure scorching through me. I don't know how he does it, how he makes me feel so freaking good. My eyes close as wave after wave of pure ecstasy passes over me. I can hear my cries, hear his name leaving my lips. Faintly. As if the voice isn't my own.

His movements slow as he drags his finger out and kisses his way down my right thigh, before he bites into the soft flesh. At the same time, he slams two fingers into my weeping pussy, sending me over the edge again. I must black out momentarily because when I open my eyes, T is staring down at me. When did he stop? When did he stand up?

"Welcome back. You good?" he asks. I don't have the strength for words so I nod my head yes to answer him. I'm better than good. I feel bloody great. "Good, because I am far from finished with you." He lifts me to my feet, spins me around, and pushes my body down on the desk. "You're going to want to hold on, dolcezza."

My arms go above my head, my fingers curling around the edge of the desk. I can feel T dragging my panties down my thighs. He lifts each foot out gently. I can hear him inhale.

"I want to bottle your fragrance, Holly. It's fucking intoxicating. I want to be able to smell your pussy at all times." I don't respond. But my body always reacts to his filthy words. My juices leak down my inner thighs as T's tongue follows the trail. I'm so sensitive. I don't know how much more I can handle, my pussy convulsing with the need to be filled by him. "Do you need something, dolcezza? All you have to do is ask?"

"I need you, T. I need you to be inside me already," I huff out.

"Well, why didn't you say so? I'd hate to leave my wife wanting for anything." I can hear his zipper being undone, the jostling of fabric, and his moans. I want to turn around. I want to see him. I go to do just that when a hand lands on my ass. The sting goes straight to my clit.

"Oh, fuck!" I grunt out as Theo simultaneously slams his cock into me.

"Fuck, I love fucking you, Holly. I could live inside this pussy 24/7. You're so fucking wet, so fucking warm, and you choke my cock so fucking good."

"Oh God, T, don't stop." I don't know if I'm begging him to keep fucking me, or to keep up the dirty talk. At this point, I think I'd come again just from the sound of his voice.

"I'm never going to stop fucking you! We'll go into the Guinness World Record book for the couple who fucks the most. Fucks the best." I push back into him in reply, meeting him thrust for thrust, doing what I can to keep up. He slams into me fast and hard. "I want you to come again, Holly. I want you to come all over my cock. I want to feel your juices running down my fucking balls. I want to bathe in your fucking juices, Holly." Holy shit... My body shakes. Goosebumps break out as a cold sweat covers me. T slows his movements. He manages to get a hand underneath me, his fingers finding my clit and pinching. "Are you going to be a good girl for me, dolcezza? Are you going to come? Drown my cock with everything you have?"

"Yes!" I scream.

T picks up his pace again, hitting that perfect spot right inside me. "Oh, fuck! I need you to come now, Holly," he grunts.

Seconds later, my whole body locks up as I come apart for him. Always for him. I've never experienced orgasms like the ones he manages to draw out of me.

His cock spills inside me, the warm liquid coating my inner walls. After a minute, he pulls out and spins me around. His lips slam down on mine, and he steals the breath right out of my lungs as he kisses me like he can't ever get enough. This man makes me feel cherished, makes me feel wanted more than I ever have before.

Chapter Thirteen

I 'm lying in bed with Holly in my arms. This is what peace is. This is what being whole is. I really would keep us in this bubble if I could. Her fingertips aimlessly run up and down my chest, tracing over my tattoos. I make a mental note to book an appointment with my artist. I need to add to my ink.

"I think I want to get one," Holly says.

"Get one what?" This woman could ask for a damn country and I'd figure out a way to buy it for her.

"A tattoo." She responds with the one thing I don't want her to get. Not because she wouldn't look good with my name inked across her skin. But unless I learn to use a tattoo gun as well as my Glock, she's not getting one.

"No," I say, immediately knowing it was the wrong choice of words. Holly picks her head up and glares at me. I see the challenge in her eyes.

"What do you mean *no*? You are not the boss of my body, T. If I want a tattoo, I'll get one."

What is it with the women in this family being so argumentative with me today? "That's where you're wrong, dolcezza." I roll her onto her back and cover her smaller frame with mine. "This body, it belongs to me. You are mine. And I'm not about to let another man touch what's mine."

She quirks an eyebrow at me. "Okay, I won't let another man touch what's yours." Well, shit, that was a little too easy... I look at her suspiciously, trying to figure out just why she'd give in without an argument. "Don't overthink, Theo. I agreed with you. My body is yours, and right now, my body is craving ice cream with chocolate sprinkles. I think it's your duty to go fetch me some." She laughs.

"You want ice cream? I'll get you a whole fucking factory." I jump to my feet and swipe a pair of discarded sweats from the floor.

"Just a bowl will suffice for now. And put a shirt on. You can't walk through the house like that. You'll give some poor girl a coronary."

I pick up a shirt and make my way down to the kitchen. I should have put some fucking shoes on. The floor's fucking cold as shit. I pull a bowl down and spoon three scoops of vanilla ice cream into it.

"Hungry?"

I turn to see a shirtless Neo enter the kitchen. "What the fuck are you doing here?" I ask. "And where the fuck are your clothes?"

"I'm using one of the guest rooms. I needed some water. Didn't think it was a crime."

"Why are you sleeping here? What's wrong with your place?"

"What's with the fucking third degree? I was tired so I crashed here. I've done it a million times before, T."

He's right. He has. But he hasn't done it when I've had a sister in the house. Fuck, I'm starting to think I was lucky, not having to grow up with the girl. I've only known about her for a short time and the amount of stress she's causing me is un-fucking-believable. "Right, well, the tap's there. You know where the glasses are." I leave him in the kitchen and walk past Angelica and Isabella's guest room.

I hear whispers and stop to listen. "Mama, are we going to see Nonno tomorrow?"

"Maybe, Izzy. We can call him in the morning,"

"Is Nonno still sad about Uncle T? Do you think that Uncle T and Nonno will make up?"

"I'm not sure, sweetheart. I don't think Nonno is sad about Uncle T. I think he's disappointed he didn't know about him all these years. That's not either of their faults," Angelica says.

"I think I love Uncle T. I want to marry someone just like him when I'm bigger," the little girl announces sternly.

Her mother laughs. "Good luck with that, Izzy. You need to marry whoever you fall in love with. Don't let anyone tell you differently. Ever, *bella*."

"Okay. Mama?"

"Yeah?"

"Do you think you'll ever fall in love?" Izzy's innocent interrogation sends a sharp pain to my chest. Is Angelica lonely? Does she need someone to be her partner in life? I never would have contemplated the idea before I met Holly.

"I think maybe I will... one day. But I have you, Izzy, and you're all the love I need." Angelica may convince her daughter, but she doesn't convince me.

I walk away. By the time I get back to the bedroom, Holly is fast asleep. I put the bowl on the nightstand and undress, before climbing in next to her. I wrap my arms around her waist and lie in silence, thanking God for sending me one of his angels. Again. I'll never stop being grateful for my wife.

"Mmm." I wake up to the best fucking feeling. I look down to a sea of red locks as Holly's head bobs up and down, her mouth a silky heaven as it captures my cock. "Fuck, dolcezza, this is how I want to wake up every day," I groan as I fist her hair and lift her head so I can see her face.

"Mhmm," she mumbles with her mouth full.

Her hand cups my balls and she starts massaging them. "Fuck, I'm going to come, Holly," I warn, but she only sucks harder, causing my spine to tingle. I come down her throat, filling her cheeks. I feel her swallow, and then, within seconds, she's jumping off the bed and running into the bathroom. What the fuck just happened? I'm left confused, until I hear her retching. I run in after her, finding her leaning over the toilet. "Fuck, shit, I'm sorry. Are you okay? What do I do? Tell me what to do, dolcezza?"

She looks up at me and laughs. "I'm fine now. Maybe hand me a glass of water."

"Should I call a doctor?" I ask as I fill a glass and pass it to her. I place my palm on her forehead. She doesn't have a fever.

"And say what? I was giving you head and threw up?"

"Well, shit. I don't know. Can't say I've ever had that reaction before..." I mutter, a little spun out and unsure what I'm supposed to do here.

"It's fine. It wasn't you. I promise. I wasn't feeling a hundred percent when I woke up. Guess I should listen to my body more."

"I'm calling a doctor." I walk back into the bedroom to retrieve my phone.

"No, you're not. Today is Sonnie's service. We are not missing this, T. I'll be fine. I probably just ate something bad—that's all."

I look her over warily. She seems okay. A little pale, but otherwise, she appears fine. Damn fucking fine. "Okay, but if you don't feel well, you tell me and we'll leave. I don't give a fuck what anyone else thinks, Holly. If you're sick, we will be seeing a doctor."

"I'll be fine. I just need a shower." Holly turns and walks back into the bathroom. She shuts the door and then I hear the water running.

That's odd. She never shuts the door. Something's obviously wrong. I reach for the handle and it's locked. She fucking locked me out. I bang my fist against the white panel. "Holly, unlock the door."

"I'm fine, T. I'm showering. Can you get me a coffee? I need caffeine."

Get her a fucking coffee? Is she serious? "Holly, open the fucking door or I'm kicking it in," I yell. I don't get an answer. I'm about to follow through with the threat, when I remember there's a fucking key sitting on the doorframe above me. I placed it there a while ago, back when I used to live here as a kid. Unlocking the handle, I push it open and step in. The steam is so thick I can't see more than two feet in front of me. What I can see is my wife sitting on the floor of the shower, the water cascading over her body as she silently sobs. "Fuck, Dolcezza, what's wrong?" I jump inside and scoop her up. Moving us back to the bench seat, I sit down with her.

"N-n-nothing's wrong," she stutters out.

I brush the wet hair from her face. "Bullshit, if nothing was wrong, you wouldn't be sitting here crying. Whatever it is, just tell me, and I'll fix it."

"You can't fix it, T. Sonnie is dead and it's all my fault. How am I-I meant to face his family today?"

"It is not your fault, Holly. Sonnie was doing his job. He knew the risks it entailed. It's not your fault. You've done nothing wrong."

"If I didn't make you take me to Italy, he'd still be here. I wouldn't have had to kill someone. I killed someone, T, and I got Sonnie killed. What kind of person does that make me?"

"Dolcezza, you are the best fucking person I've ever met. You are not to blame for what happened. If anyone is to blame, it's me. I took you with me, knowing full well the situation we were walking into. I should have been there to protect you, to make sure nothing like that ever happened to you."

"What-what's going to happen now? Is it even safe to go to this service today? Should we be out in public like that?"

Lana's warning from yesterday replays in my mind. I shove it down. "Nothing will happen. We will be surrounded by my men, dolcezza. I'll make sure you're safe."

"And you? I need to know that you'll be safe, T."

"I promise you I will always do whatever I have to

do to stay safe. To return to you. You are my shining light, always showing me the way home. You lead me out of the darkness, Holly."

"What if I'm the one needing the light? What if I'm drowning in a darkness of my own, T? I killed someone and I'd do it again if I had to."

"Good. You need to always choose yourself. Don't ever hesitate, Holly."

"I feel like a hypocrite," she mumbles.

"Why?" My hands stroke up and down her back, trying to offer her whatever comfort I can.

"I blamed my dad for killing that man. I hated him. I told him he was a monster. He never showed any remorse for what he did. And look at me... I'm just like him. I don't feel remorse. I was fucking relieved."

"You were young, Holly. Your dad does not blame you for thinking that." I sigh. "Let me ask you this. Do you think I'm a monster? Do you think less of me for the things I've done? Because I can guarantee you I've done things far worse than you could ever imagine, dolcezza."

She mulls over my question, not saying anything for a while, and I wonder if she hasn't really ever considered the things I'm capable of doing. "I think that you are some people's monster. The boogeyman that keeps them awake at night. But to me, you're the one thing that helps me sleep. You are the one person I can trust wholeheartedly to always have my back. You are a part of me, like we are not two separate people anymore."

"We're united, Holly. We will reign over this city together. We will build our own legacy for our children and children's children."

"A united reign. I like it." She smiles.

"Me too."

Chapter Fourteen

Holly

T went downstairs to make a few calls and left me to get ready. I've chosen a black lace dress. It seems funeral appropriate, although it does cling to my curves and the cut around my breasts gives me the appearance of having more cleavage than I actually do. I like it though. I've applied light makeup, trying to keep it as natural as possible, and left my hair hanging down my back in loose curls.

I walk into the closet to find shoes. I still don't

know how T manages to have wardrobes filled with clothes and accessories for me no matter where we are. I'll have to remember to ask him about it. I select a pair of black Jimmy Choo heels and snap a photo of my feet to send to Reilly later. She loves a good designer shoe— well, a designer anything really.

I've never cared too much about labels before, or my appearance for that matter. But I don't want to embarrass T by seeming like anything less than someone deserving of him. I know... I shouldn't be dressing to impress him or anyone else. However, I can't lie and say I don't enjoy the way he looks at me, the way his eyes darken and fill with lust when he runs them up and down my body.

I head downstairs to find him, but run into one of his men instead. I can't remember the guy's name. I've been trying not to make eye contact with any of them ever since Sonnie died. Do they blame me? Did they know him? Were they friends? All these questions run through my mind as I look at this man, dressed in an all-black suit with a scary-looking scowl on his face. "Mrs. Valentino, are you okay?" he asks.

"Uh, yeah. Have you, um, have you seen T or Neo?"

"They're both in the boss's office, ma'am."

"Thank you, and it's just Holly. You can call me Holly."

He laughs a little before he recovers with a cough in his hand. "I don't think the boss would appreciate that too much, Mrs. Valentino."

"Well, he might not, but I sure would. Mrs. Valentino makes me sound old. *Ma'am* makes me sound ancient. Neither option is one I want to feel." I give him my sweetest smile before I pivot in the direction of my husband's office.

I'm stopped by two more beefy guards standing in front of the closed doors. "Sorry, boss is busy. You can't go in there," one of them says.

"Busy? Doing what?" I fold my arms over my chest. I don't miss how his slimy eyes go straight to my cleavage, which has me dropping my fists by my side.

"He's in a meeting, ma'am."

Argh, again with the *ma'am*. I'm starting to think I look way older than I bloody well am. "Okay, well, I'm going in there, so unless you're prepared to physically stop me from entering that office, I would appreciate it if you would step aside."

One of the guards, the one who's been a quiet observer, slides out of my way. However, his counterpart doesn't budge. "Sorry, ma'am, I can't let you in."

I look to the other guard; he's watching the beefy one blocking the doorway like he's looking at a stranger. "I'm assuming you have a gun on you somewhere, right?" I ask my newly appointed ally. He nods his head. "Good, I'm going to need to borrow it." I hold out a palm. He hesitates slightly before he hands over what I'm assuming is a Glock. I don't actually know the difference, but I do remember that T taught me how to use one that looks just like this.

Flipping the safety off, I aim at the beefcake's shoe

and press the trigger. It's easier than I thought. I'm sure he won't die from a bullet through the foot—at least, I hope he won't. He screams out in pain. "What the fuck? Are you crazy?" he yells.

"You know, I think maybe I am a little unhinged right now. If you ever try to stop me from seeing my husband again, the next bullet will be between your bloody eyes, mate," I seethe, right as the doors swing open.

T and Neo both exit with their guns drawn. "Fucking hell, that's one way to make yourself known, Little Queen." Neo laughs.

"Get him out of here," T orders the guard who's still standing. I watch as the man nods, then lifts his friend to his feet.

He's about to walk off when I stop him. "Wait, here. This is yours. Thank you." I hand him his gun back. "T, I think *that one* needs a raise," I say as they're both walking away.

Theo doesn't respond. He looks me over, silently assessing my body from head to toe. "Are you hurt anywhere?" he asks.

"No?" My reply comes out more as a question than a statement.

"Good. Care to explain why you're running around shooting at our guards?"

"One guard, Theo. I shot one guard... not guards. And he wasn't going to let me in. I wanted to see you." I shrug as I walk past him and Neo to enter the office. I haven't really spent much time in here, but it's a nice room. The windows overlook a maze of winding hedges.

"I think you've created a fucking menace to society, coz." Neo laughs.

I turn to look at him. "I'm not a menace. I just don't like being told I can't see my husband when I need to. What was so important that I couldn't *enter*..." I use air quotes to emphasize the word. "...the office?"

"Nothing," they both answer at the same time, which tells me it was definitely not nothing.

"Really? Nothing?" I walk to the desk and look over the scattered papers. They appear to be business reports, boring and full of terminology I don't even understand. "Well, maybe let your guard dogs know that next time," I tell them. They're both staring at me, not saying a word. "What?" I'm getting frustrated with the silence.

"Who are you, and what did you do to Holly? Shit, do we need Father Thomas to come and do an exorcism? Are you possessed?" Neo asks, and I think he's actually serious.

"Please tell me you don't believe that could possibly happen?"

"Why couldn't it? Spirits are all around us, Holly," he counters.

"If that were the case, don't you think you two would be having way worse lives? You know, with the spirits of all the people you've... you know... hanging around."

"Okay, that's enough of this conversation. Neo,

stop being an idiot or I'll hand her a gun and let her shoot you again. She seems to have developed a trigger-happy finger." T smirks as he approaches to wrap his arm around me. "Are you sure you're okay?" he whispers into my hair.

"I am now." I lean into him, inhaling his scent. It's soothing. I'm not going to tell him that I still feel nauseous as hell. I just need to get through the day. I'm sure it's stress and grief. I haven't processed that Sonnie is really gone. Today seems to make it much more tangible. I didn't even know him for that long, but I liked him. I thought we'd be friends for years to come.

"Okay, let's go." T takes my hand and I follow him outside, where a convoy awaits our arrival. He opens the back door of the SUV smack-bang in the middle and helps me climb in. Neo gets in on the other side, and T slides in next to me. He twists his fingers around mine, bringing my hand to his mouth, then he kisses each knuckle. "It's going to be okay," he whispers, almost like a prayer. Is he trying to reassure me or himself?

The service was huge. It seems I wasn't the only one who liked Sonnie. His mum came up and hugged me. She said her son had spoken very highly of me. I cried with her, apologizing for her loss, for everyone's loss. The burial followed right after the service.

As I let T lead me back to the car, I can't help but wonder how many times I'm going to have to watch a casket being lowered into the ground. "How many funerals have you been to?" I ask Theo. In just the few months I've known him, this was the third I've had to sit through. I'm counting his own, even if I knew it was fake at the time.

"Ah, a few." He kisses the side of my head as he inspects our surroundings. He's been on high alert ever since we left the house, and we seem to have twice as many men guarding us lately.

When he stops, all the men in suits move closer to us. "Is something wrong?" I press, looking around while trying to see if something feels off.

"No, it's fine, dolcezza." He smiles tightly before facing Neo and barking out a long string of Italian. They're speaking back and forth so quickly that I have no chance of understanding what they're saying.

The more I watch and listen to them, the angrier I'm getting. I try to pull away from Theo, only to have him tighten his grip on my arm. "Stop! You're hurting me. And stop speaking in Italian. If something is going on, I want to bloody know about it," I curse at him, yanking my arm away.

"Cazzo!" T sighs. "There's been a change of plans. We're going this way. Neo will meet us on the other side of the cemetery."

"Why?" I ask, jogging in an attempt to keep up with his long, fast strides.

"No reason. I just wanted to walk for a bit."

"Yeah, and I'm Mary bloody Poppins. Don't lie to me, Theo."

"Okay, there was a car parked across the road—it wasn't one of ours. It belongs to the Gambinos. They shouldn't be here."

"See? Was that so hard?" I can't help but sass him.

"Yes, it was, actually. All I want to do is protect you, Holly. You make that fucking hard to do sometimes."

"Yeah, well, you're making a lot of things harder than they need to be. All you have to do is tell me. Stop treating me like I'm a fragile piece of glass. I'm not going to break on you, T."

"I know you're not going to break. You are stronger than any made man I've ever met, dolcezza."

"Thank—" *Oh shit...* My hand tries to tighten around his. The ground beneath me starts spinning, and then I'm falling...

"Fuck!" I faintly hear Theo shout. Who's he yelling at?

Chapter Fifteen

"Why the fuck isn't she waking up? What the fuck is wrong with her? Someone better do something real fucking soon, before I blow a hole through all of your useless fucking brains." I pick up a water pitcher and throw it against the wall.

"Mr. Valentino, she will wake up. All the scans came up with nothing. She fainted. It's common. We just need to give her body time to recover."

"It's not fucking common to faint and not come back to. It's been an hour. She should be awake by now. What kind of cereal box did you get your degree from? Fucking useless. Neo, find a fucking doctor who knows what he's doing."

"T, you need to calm the fuck down. Listen to me. She's going to wake up any minute now. Just give it a bit of time," Neo says.

"Time? Fuck off with your time. I want her to wake up now! She needs to fucking wake up." At this point, I don't even know who I'm yelling at. When Holly fainted in the cemetery, I caught her, ran to the fucking car, and rushed her to the closest ER. These useless fucks have done nothing but put her through some scan machines, and they're telling me that she'll wake up when she's ready. Fuck that. I'm not waiting around for these fuckers to get their thumbs out of their fucking asses. "Fine, if no one else will do it, I'll do it my damn self." I whip my phone out of my pocket and call the family doc.

He answers on the first ring—that's what we fucking pay him for. "Boss, what's up?"

"It's Holly. She fainted and she's not fucking waking up, Doc. We're in the ER and all these useless fucking assholes aren't doing a damn thing to help her."

"Okay, what hospital?"

"The Presbyterian."

"I'll be right there. Theo, don't do anything stupid. I'm sure they're doing all they can."

"Yeah, well, *all they can* isn't fucking enough," I yell as I hang up the phone.

"T, what's wrong?" I spin around, almost afraid I'm completely losing my fucking mind. But lying in the bed, with her bright green eyes wide open while struggling to sit herself up, is Holly. Awake.

"Thank fucking God! Don't ever fucking do that to me again," I say as I push her back down. "Don't get up. Lie still."

"What? Why? Where am I?" She looks around the room.

"You're in the hospital. You passed out, Holly. You've been out of it for an hour. A whole fucking hour and the fucking idiot doctors couldn't do a damn thing to wake you up."

"Mr. Valentino, we need to check her over," a doctor interjects from behind me.

"T, I'm fine. Look, I'm awake and right here. I'm sorry. I don't know what happened."

"It's not your fault." I lean down and kiss her forehead. Pivoting on my heel, I give the doctor my iciest glare. "I want every fucking test you can possibly run. I want to know why the fuck she passed out for a fucking hour." I thought we were in the clear with this fainting nonsense after we got her over her fear of guns.

"Okay, if you'll give us the room, we can examine her."

I look at him, tilting my head while trying to determine if the asshole is brave or stupid. I'm going with stupid. "He can stay. He has to stay," Holly speaks up, reaching out and grabbing hold of my hand before I can say anything the son of a bitch is likely to regret.

"Okay, what about him?" The man gestures towards Neo.

Holly looks to me, unsure what she should do. "Neo, can you get her something to eat and some decent fucking coffee."

He glances from me to Holly and nods. "Call me if he gets out of hand, Holly." He smirks and leaves the room.

"Okay, Mrs. Valentino, how are you feeling?" Dr. Dimwit asks.

"What kind of fucking question is that? She's been passed out for over an hour. How do you think she's feeling?" I growl.

"T, stop. Let the doctor do his job so I can go home."

"Home? You're not going home, dolcezza. They need to run all sorts of tests and shit."

"I'm fine. I feel fine. I have a headache, and I'm slightly nauseous. But other than that, I'm fine."

"When was the last time you ate, Mrs. Valentino?"

"Ah, last night," Holly answers, and I curse myself for not making sure she fucking ate breakfast before we left the house. From now on, I'll make sure she fucking eats every meal.

"When was your last menstrual cycle?"

Okay, now I really want to shoot fucking Dr. Dimwit. That's a personal fucking question, and frankly, none of his fucking business. But as I'm racking my brain, trying to remember myself, I'm coming up empty. I look to Holly, waiting for her answer. "Um, I'm not sure," she says quietly, as if she's still thinking.

"Is there any chance you could be pregnant?" Doctor Dimwit continues.

"Yes," I say at the same time Holly says, "No."

"Dolcezza, I'm not sure if anybody ever told you about the birds and the bees, but when you do things, things that you and I happen to do really fucking well..." I smirk at the redness creeping up her cheeks. "...you tend to, you know, get pregnant."

"I know how the birds and the bees work, idiot." She frowns at me. "I'm not pregnant. I can't be. I'm not ready to be pregnant."

"Right, well, I'll have a test run just to rule it out then. Sometimes these things don't happen when we're ready, Mrs. Valentino."

"I'm not pregnant," Holly says more sternly. I reach behind my back, making sure my Glock is well and truly out of her reach, because with the way she's staring daggers at this guy, I wouldn't put it past her to shoot him.

"Right, I'll send the nurse in with a test in a minute. All other scans were clear. There is no medical reason for your sudden fainting. I'd put it down to your nausea and the fact you haven't eaten in over fourteen or so hours."

"Thank you," I grit out as politely as I can manage. I'm fucking fuming that I had been so inattentive to her needs this morning. I wait for the doctor to leave the room before I turn to Holly. I can't help the huge grin that I'm sporting. My eyes go straight to her midsection, straight to where my son very well could be growing right now.

I put my hand on her stomach, and she instantly shoves it off. "Stop it. I'm not bloody pregnant."

"Well, I think you could be. We have a lot of unprotected sex, Holly."

"I also take the pill—every day."

"You haven't missed any? At all? Not one?" I ask, curious. She thinks about it, and the moment realization sinks in, she pales. "Shit, Holly, it's okay. It will be okay."

"It won't be. I missed pills. When you died... when I thought you were gone, I didn't take anything for a week, T. A whole week. We had sex that week."

"Dolcezza, you being pregnant is not a bad thing. Us, starting our family, that's a good thing, yeah?" I'm not understanding why she's so freaked out. I'm fucking ecstatic at the thought of Holly being knocked up with my kid.

"I'm not ready, T. We need more time. We need time to just be us. We haven't had enough time. And I'm going to get fat! Really fat. And a baby? How am I meant to look after a baby? I can barely look after myself right now."

"You are not in this alone. We will get through it all. Together. United, remember? You and I are a fucking package deal, Holly. Whatever happens, I'll do everything to make it as easy for you as I can."

"I'm going to get fat," she repeats.

"Holly, you're not going to get fat. You'll be growing our son. There is nothing more fucking beautiful than that."

"I'm not ready, T. I don't know if I can do this."

"We will do this. You will be fine. I'll make sure of it. You are going to make the best fucking mother, dolcezza."

Tears stream down her cheeks. "I'm scared, Theo. What do I know about kids?"

I laugh, much to her disappointment. "Holly, you're a teacher. I'd say you know a lot about kids. More than I do."

The door to the room opens, and a nurse walks in. "Okay, sweetheart, I just need you to pee in this cup for me." Holly's hands shake as she takes the plastic container from the older woman. "Are you okay, sweetheart? Do you need me to get you anything?" The nurse glances between us, giving me a very disapproving look.

"I'm okay, just shocked I guess."

"Come on, dolcezza, I'll help you." I pull her up, holding on to her until I'm sure she has her footing.

"You're not watching me pee, T." Holly tries to push me out of the way.

"I'm coming in that bathroom with you, Holly. We are doing this together, the whole way, and it all starts with you peeing in that cup. I'm not fucking missing that."

Holly groans as she grabs my hand and tugs me into the bathroom. "Turn the tap on. I need some encouragement. If you're watching, I'm not going to be able to pee," she says as she slides her panties down and sits on the toilet.

"You know, I've been up close and personal with all those parts." I point to her crotch area. "A little bit of pee is nothing, dolcezza."

"Just be quiet," she mumbles as she closes her eyes.

She pees, flushes the toilet, and washes her hands. "What now?" she asks, staring at the cup on the counter.

I pick up the plastic container and open the door. "Here you go. How does this work? How long do we have to wait?" I ask the nurse while attempting to pass over the sample.

"Not too long. Just place it on the counter here. The doctor will be in shortly." I do as I'm instructed and hold Holly's hand. The woman smiles and dons a pair of disposable gloves, before collecting everything and walking out the door. Holly and I sit down and wait in silence.

Ten minutes later a doctor walks through the door. "Holly Valentino?" he asks.

"Yes." Holly's voice is shaky, quiet.

"Congratulations, you're pregnant." The older man grins tentatively.

I mentally give myself a high-five. She's pregnant.

With my kid. "Holy shit, we're pregnant. We are actually having a baby. A piece of you and a piece of me. I fucking love you, Holly." I pick her up and spin her around before I remember the baby.

She's fucking pregnant. *Holy shit, she's pregnant.* What the fuck do I do now? Does she need a doctor? Should they be checking on the baby? She did faint... Fuck, I need some information on pregnancy. I have no idea what to do, how to help her.

We listen to all the "dos and don'ts" the doctor is informing us on—well, I listen and Holly zones out, pretending to listen. There're appointments that need to be set up. After I thank the older man and assure him we'll be seeing the best OB-GYN money can buy, he leaves. Then I turn to my wife, who is clearly still in shock.

Chapter Sixteen

Pregnant. The one word that changes everything keeps flashing through my mind. This is what I've always wanted. What I've always dreamed of: finding a husband, settling down, having children. I may not have the white picket fence and the safe, boring husband, but I wouldn't swap T for anyone in the world. I want his children. Of course I want his children.

Why the hell am I not over the moon about this? I

look at Theo, who hasn't been able to wipe the smile off his face since we found out about our impending doom. No, not doom... our impending bundle of joy. *This is a blessing.* I need to start thinking of it that way. And stop thinking that it's the end of life as I know it.

I should call Reilly. She always knows what to say to get me out of my own head. And that's all this is. I'm stuck in my own negative mindset. I love kids. I'm a teacher—of course I love kids. I can't for the life of me figure out what my hang-ups about this are. I love my husband, and I know he loves me. And I know that he will be a great dad.

"Here, drink this." I mindlessly take the hot cup of coffee from T and sip, which very quickly comes flying back out of my mouth.

"What the bloody hell is this?" I ask, inspecting the cup. It looks like coffee; it smells like coffee. But it's certainly *not* coffee.

"It's decaf. I just read that you can't drink caffeine while you're pregnant, so I had all the coffee in the house thrown out," T says proudly.

"You what? Oh, Lord. Please, someone tell me I'm on some prank show and you're joking. You are joking, right?"

"Nope. I'm fully invested in doing this pregnancy thing with you. If you can't drink caffeine, then neither can I."

"T, you literally have a house full of Italians. Italians who are very freaking fond of their coffee."

"They can get it elsewhere." He shrugs like it's no big deal.

"Argh, nope. I cannot give up coffee. I won't. No way."

"We will do this together, dolcezza."

"Easy for you to say. You're not the one who's going to be the size of a house and pushing something the size of a watermelon out your vagina."

He visibly shudders and screws his face up. "What are your thoughts on C-sections?"

I send him my best *don't fuck with me* glare.

"Kidding. It'll be fine. Your body is designed to handle this, Holly."

"Argh, shoot me now!" I groan. This is going to be the longest nine months of my freaking life. I watch T walk over to the bar and pour a glass of whiskey. I smile at the pain I'm about to inflict on him. I stand, take the glass from him, and pour the whiskey back into the decanter. "You can't drink alcohol. We're pregnant, remember? Pregnant people can't drink alcohol."

He blinks a few times before he smiles. "Fine, I don't need it anyway. A nine-month cleanse will be good for me."

I throw myself on the sofa and lean my head back.

"What's wrong? Are you feeling okay? Do you need something to eat? I'll get you some food."

"T, stop! You're driving me bloody insane, and it's been three hours. Just stop hovering, and go and do whatever it is you do. I'm sure you've got work to do," I yell at him.

He sits down, plucks me up, and positions me on his lap. "I get that you're not exactly thrilled about this news, Holly. I'm really trying hard to fucking understand why you don't want kids with me. But you can't ask me to not want to take care of you. You can try to shut me out; you can yell at me all you like. But I'm still going to be right here. With you. I'm still going to love this child who's part you, part me. I'm still going to love you with every fiber of my being."

I start bawling my eyes out into his chest. "I'm sorry. I love you. I don't know what's wrong with me." I take a breath. "It's not that I don't want a child with you. I do. I just... I don't know what's wrong with me."

"Dolcezza, nothing is wrong with you. You are allowed to feel how you feel. I know this is a shock. We didn't exactly plan it. We didn't really try too hard to prevent it either, but that's not the point. The point is: if you need time to come to terms, well, I'd say you have around seven months... give or take."

"We're going to have a baby, and we don't even have a house. Not really. Not yet, T. I don't have a job. I don't have my sister or my mum. I was meant to have Reilly here for this. We were meant to have kids together. Who's going to come and babysit for me, when I want to take a long bath, or literally do anything else?"

"Trust me, you're going to have a hard time keeping this baby in your arms, Holly. Have you met my mother? She's going to be so overbearing you'll want to scream at her. Besides, when you want a few hours of peace, I'll take him shooting or something. You know, teach him young."

I sit up. *He'll take him shooting.* Oh shit, why didn't I think of this before? Our child is going to follow in Theo's footsteps. He'll be born into a life of crime.

"I'm kidding, Holly. It was a joke. Obviously a bad one. I promise I will not take a baby shooting."

"What about when he's older? Is our child going to have to join the *family* business, like you did?"

"No, absolutely not. I'd be lying if I said I wouldn't want a successor. But no child of mine will ever be forced into this life, Holly. You have my word on that."

"Okay, thank you. What if they want to be an accountant, or a hairdresser, or a dancer, or something? That would be okay, right? They don't have to turn into a mobster."

"A mobster? That's what you think I am?" T laughs.

"Well, aren't you?"

"I'm a businessman, Holly. I run many multimillion-dollar companies."

"Right," I draw out. T stands with me still in his arms. "What are you doing? Put me down."

"Nope, I'm going to run you a bath. You need to relax for a bit."

I've been soaking in this bath for almost thirty minutes. The water is cold. But the book I'm reading has allowed me to escape into a fairy-tale world—one with fae, werewolves, and witches. I don't know where T managed to find this Kindle, but I almost burst into tears again when he brought it to me.

Deciding it's been long enough, I jump out and wrap a towel around myself. I find my phone on the bedside table and flop down on the bed. Taking a breath, I dial Reilly. I'm about to hang up when she answers. "Holly, where have you been? I've been trying to call for hours. Something's wrong. I can feel it. And tell that husband of yours to answer my bloody calls too."

"Ah, we were in the hospital. I think our phones might have been turned off," I lie. I saw her trying to call, but I told T not to answer it.

"What do you mean you were in the hospital? What happened? I knew something was wrong. But Bray wouldn't believe me."

"I, uh, I fainted. That's all. I'm fine though."

"Okay, and now, how about the truth? You know you can't bullshit me, Holly." I don't say anything in response. What do I say? How do I say this? "Holly, unless you want me to jump on a flight right now, you best start speaking. Whose grave am I digging?"

"That's not funny, Rye. It's not that bad. It's just... I-I, um, I'm pregnant," I stutter out. Silence, I'm met with silence. I pull the phone away to see if we lost the connection. "Rye? Are you there?"

"Yeah... OMG, Holly, you're pregnant. Like having a baby kind of pregnant?"

"I'm not sure there's any other kind, Rye."

"Holy shit, I'm going to be an auntie!"

"You already are an auntie. Remember Ash? The baby Alyssa just had." I laugh.

"Yeah, but that's different. She's not my twin sister. My sister is having a baby. I'm so happy for you, Holly. This is what you've always wanted."

"Yeah, it is." I sigh.

"Wait, are you not happy? What's wrong? Did that husband of yours do something stupid? I don't care if he's meant to be some big, scary mob boss. I will cut his dick off."

"No, T's... Well, he's bloody perfect. He's ecstatic, if not over-the-top overbearing already."

"Good, he should be. But what's going on, Holly?"

"I don't know, Rye. I'm scared. What if I'm not a good mum? What if I can't love this baby? Maybe all my love was already given to Theo. I love him so much I can't breathe sometimes. How can I possibly have any love left to offer?"

"Holly, you are going to be the best mother this world has ever seen. You are the most loving person I know. If anyone has enough love to go around, it's you. I've always envied your ability to connect with people, to really care about causes others wouldn't blink an eye at. There is not a doubt in my mind that you are going to be just fine. Your baby is already one of the luckiest kids in the world."

"How so?" I ask, sniffling.

"He, or she, has two parents who love each other. Two parents who connect on such a deep level it's almost sickening to watch. But he, or she, also has me as their favorite auntie, and they really can't be any luckier than that." She laughs.

"You're right... I'm worrying about nothing."

"I'm always right! You're worrying because you already care. You already love this baby. You just haven't let yourself feel it yet."

"Thank you."

"Anytime. I love you, Hol."

"Love you more." I hang up, the weight on my shoulders lighter.

"Feel better?" T steps out of the shadows of the corner of the room, making me jump six feet in the air.

"Jesus bloody hell, T, how long have you been standing there?" I ask.

"Long enough." He comes over and cups my face in his palms.

"I fucking love the shit out of you, Holly Valentino."

"I love you more, Theo Valentino."

"Impossible, dolcezza."

131

Chapter Seventeen

I know I shouldn't have been listening in on Holly's conversation with her sister, but fuck... I needed to know what she was thinking. She wasn't opening up to me like she does with her twin. Does that piss me off? Yes, but I also understand the connection those two share is stronger than a normal sibling bond. Hearing Holly say she was scared she wouldn't be able to love her own child because she thinks all her love is used up on me, well, that just about broke me.

She doesn't realize just how fucking perfect she is. She's a fucking angel. I smirk, staring at the soldier currently strung up in my warehouse. Maybe she's a little dark these days, but she's still heaven-sent. I didn't want to leave Holly back at the house today, but these loose ends need to be tied. I won't have any fucker around with a vendetta against her. "You disrespected my wife. You disrespected me," I say calmly as I remove my tie, then my shirt.

"N-no, Boss I didn't. I was following orders. You said not to let anyone in."

"And you thought that included my wife?"

"You said *anyone*."

"Tsk, tsk, tsk. Being stupid does not bode well for folks in our industry."

"It won't happen again. I swear it won't."

"You're right. It won't. Ya see, I had a lot of pent-up anger today. I was looking forward to dragging this out. But I have much more important things to do." He doesn't speak in return, just nods up and down like a bobble head. "I watched the security feed, you know. I saw the way you leered at my wife. She's hot, right? It's hard not to look at her."

"N-no."

"No? Are you telling me my wife isn't hot?" I ask him. There's no right answer to this. I know it; he knows it.

"Yes, she is. No... I mean, I don't know, boss."

Without a word, I stalk forward and dig my thumbs into his eye sockets and scoop back until the optic nerves are hanging loose. "Nobody disrespects my wife," I hiss into his ear. "Finish it," I tell Neo, and I hear two shots as I walk out of the room. I'm stopped in front of the warehouse. There's a convoy of blacked-out SUVs lined up the street, and one Al fucking Donatello standing smack dab in front of me.

"I trust he deserved to have his eyes gouged out." He smirks at me, his eyes twinkling with something I can't read.

I shrug. "I've done much worse for much less. What are you doing here?" I glance towards the army of soldiers he has with him, and smile. The old man must be afraid of me, or my reaction to seeing him. Lucky for him, Isabella appears fond of the son of a bitch, which means, for her sake, I'll let him live. For now.

"We need to talk. Not here. Get in." He points to the car closest to him.

I laugh. "Yeah, that's not happening. You want to talk, follow me. If you can keep up." I don't look back as I jump into my Maserati, enjoying the purr of the engine as I floor it away from the warehouse. I head back to my parents' estate. Absentmindedly. I shouldn't have brought him here, but this is where Holly is, so this is where I want to be. I wait on the front steps as Donatello's convoy pulls up behind me. "You can come in, but your goons have to wait out here."

I watch him nod to one of his men, and they all hop back into their respective vehicles. Rose, one of the housemaids, approaches me as we enter the foyer. "Good evening, sir, can I get you anything?"

"Show Mr. Donatello to the study," I instruct her. "I'll meet you there shortly. I have someone I need to see first." I jog up the stairs towards my old bedroom. It feels disrespectful to the man who raised me to have Donatello in his house. I don't even know if my pops knew the truth.

Holly's asleep, all curled up in the blankets. I lean down and brush the hair off her face, kissing her forehead lightly. She stirs but doesn't open her eyes. Walking out, I close the door quietly and make my way back to the study.

"Right, so what was so urgent you couldn't say it over the phone?" I ask, entering the study to find not only Donatello, but also Neo and his old man.

"Uncle Gabe, I didn't know you were stopping by." I haven't heard much from him since returning to the city. He was my father's consigliere, now mine. Not that I'm really sure I'm too capable of taking advice anyway.

"Yeah, your mother asked me to stop by," he says, eyeing Donatello warily.

"Did everyone but me fucking know about this? Did Pops know?" I ask, not missing the flinch in Donatello's face.

"Yes, he did. And he loved you like his own anyway," my uncle grunts back.

Yeah, that does not make me feel any fucking better about the situation. "Well, as you can see, I'm a busy man. Tell me what you need to say and then get the fuck out of my house."

"It's the Clover. He's in town, and word is he's building up an army, looking to exterminate the entire Valentino bloodline."

"That's it? In case you haven't fucking noticed, the whole of New York is currently hoping to do the same. Not exactly news."

"From what I hear, there are only two families still talking shit. The Garzos are too busy looking for their boss. Know anything about that?"

"Nope," I answer, letting the 'P' pop.

"That's what I thought. Hal Gambino is also MIA... Guess you don't know anything about that either?"

"Good guess and good riddance."

"His sons are out for blood. They know you had something to do with it."

I laugh. Hal's sons are nothing but rich playboy wannabes. "Let them come at me."

"Right, anyone ever tell you you're too cocky for your own good?" Donatello asks.

"Yeah. My father. All the fucking time." I smirk.

"Right. Anyway, the Clover AKA Noah Kelly and Big Johnno flew in from Italy a week ago. They've been here for days, without a peep. They're not stupid, T. They are planning something big. These are not men you want lurking in the shadows with your family in the crosshairs. You need to be on the offensive. You should send your wife and mother somewhere safe."

"My wife goes where I go. Sending her anywhere is out of the question. As for my mother, she'll be fine wherever she is."

"You're a stubborn son of a bitch, and it's going to get you killed."

I'm about to tell him to go fuck himself when a little voice stops me in my tracks. "Nonno, I knew I heard you. What are you doing here? Did you know Uncle T and Aunt Holly bought a new house? And they're having a baby."

I look down at Isabella, now standing beside me, having squeezed her hand in mine. "How'd you know about that?" I ask.

She shrugs. "I hear things. And now I'm going to be a cousin. Isn't that good, Nonno?"

"It's great, Izzy. Bellissimo. Congratulations," Donatello says, while Uncle Gabe and Neo stare at me in shock. I hadn't gotten around to telling them (or anyone) yet.

"I hope it's a girl cousin. Do you think it will be a girl cousin, Uncle T?" Izzy asks me.

"I'm not sure, *bella*. But whatever kind of cousin it is, I'm sure they will be thrilled to meet you. Why don't you go find your mother? It's getting late."

"But I just got in here." She pouts.

"Bel, come with me. Let's raid Uncle T's fridge. I think we need cake," Neo says, picking her up and throwing her over his shoulder.

"Yes, cake! Bye, Nonno. Ti voglio bene," she squeals as they exit the room.

"She seems like she's at home here," Donatello observes.

"She is." I shrug.

"Angelica said you'd accepted them in, no questions asked. I'm glad. They were both excited about you."

"We're not here for some big family reunion. You came to warn me. You've done that. Now, if you'll excuse me, I have shit to do." I stop at the door. "Uncle Gabe, tell my mother she should come home." As angry as I am at her right now, I'd never forgive myself if something happened to her. I head straight back to the bedroom and shower quickly before slipping into bed with my wife. Resting my hand on her stomach, I send up a silent prayer that we make it through this fucking shitshow of a war. I may not have drawn first blood, but I will fucking draw the last. I will make sure Holly and our child are safe.

I wake up to an empty bed. Again. I jump straight up, about to walk out of the bedroom in search of Holly, when I hear her in the bathroom. I push the door open and see her pale face bent over the toilet. I sit down next to her and pull her hair away from her face. "This is your fault, you know. You did this to me," she says, leaning against my chest.

"Yeah, I did!" I mentally high-five myself again. I got Holly knocked up. "What can I do? How can I help?"

"You can't." She jumps over to the bowl again and is emptying what little she has left in her stomach.

"I should call Doc. This can't be good, right? What if something's wrong?" I start to panic.

"T, something *is* wrong with me. It's called pregnancy. I'll be fine. I'm sure it will pass. Could you get me some water, and my toothbrush?"

I kiss her forehead, ignoring the scent of vomit she currently has going on. I've smelt worse bodily fluids. I pour a glass of water and squirt some toothpaste onto her toothbrush. "Here, open up," I say, holding the toothbrush to her mouth.

She screws her face up at me and snatches the brush out of my hand. "You are not brushing my teeth. I'm not an invalid."

"No, but you are mine. If I want to help you brush your teeth, I will."

"Nope, not happening." She stands and leans on the counter as she brushes her teeth. I flush the toilet and close the lid so I can take a seat and watch her.

"You are seriously the most beautiful creature I've ever seen. You know that?" I tell her honestly. She's standing there, wearing nothing but one of my shirts. I can see the swell of her breasts, her nipples poking at the cotton. The long red mass of curls hangs freely down her back.

"Really, right now? That's your thought process? I'm covered in sweat, and I stink like a bucket of prawns in the sun."

"It doesn't matter. You're still the most beautiful thing I've ever seen."

"Thanks?" she questions.

"Come on, put some pants on." I look her over. "And a bra. You need to try to eat something."

"Really, why do I need to get dressed to go eat breakfast?" she complains.

"Because I don't feel like gouging the eyes out of every fucking soldier under my employ when they can't help but stare at you, which they sure as fuck will if you walk out wearing just that shirt."

Holly rolls her eyes. "You wouldn't gouge their eyes out for looking at me. That's a tad dramatic and psychotic, T."

"Well, dolcezza, I guess you're married to a dramatic, psychotic man." I slap her ass and lead her into the closet.

Chapter Eighteen

Holly

T and I walk into the dining room, hand in hand. I feel like absolute crap still and would much rather be in bed. The space is full of people. Angelica and Isabella, Neo and his dad, and Gloria. I do a double take. T's mum is here. She jumps up and practically runs to us. I drop his hand, thinking she's going for him, but to my surprise, she wraps her arms around me. She says something in a string of Italian that I have no chance of understanding.

"Ma, English," Theo snaps.

"It's fine. I like the way it sounds." I shrug when Gloria pulls back.

"Thank you." She kisses me on both cheeks before moving to her son and offering the same. "Theo, you look skinny. You need to eat. Come, sit," she demands.

It's nice to be surrounded by family, although I can't help but wish for Reilly to be here. It would have been nice to have her help me furniture shop for the new house. She would have loved it.

"What are your plans today, Holly? We should go to the spa. You deserve to relax and be pampered."

"Have the spa come to the house, Ma. You can't go out today," T answers before I can.

"Why can't I go out?" I argue. You'd think he'd know by now that when he says I can't do something, it only makes me want to do it so much more.

"Because I said so. No one is leaving the house today." Theo looks around the table. "We will talk about this later," he says into my ear. I don't bother arguing or giving him the piece of my mind that I want to. I'll wait until we're behind closed doors. Instead, I dig into the pile of food he placed in front of me. The nausea seems to have passed and I'm absolutely starving.

"Izzy and I are going back to Italy tonight," Angelica says, breaking the silence.

T snaps his head up. "Are you sure that's safe?"

Angelica shrugs. "Izzy has school. I can't keep her away forever."

"So, get her school to send her work. She can do it from here," he commands.

"Theo, she needs stability, her friends, teachers. I'm not homeschooling her."

"I can help. I mean, if you wanted to stay longer. I can help her with her schoolwork," I offer. It's not like I have anything else to do. I also have a feeling T is either not ready for them to leave, or there's another reason he wants them to stay. Either way, I will always back my husband one hundred percent. His hand lands on my knee under the table.

"See, it's settled. Holly happens to be the best teacher I know." T smiles proudly.

"I'm the only teacher you know. Right?"

"Doesn't matter. Still the best, dolcezza."

"Fine, I'll call her school and find out what arrangements can be made. But this isn't an indefinite solution. We will have to return to Italy eventually."

"Sure," T agrees with Angelica. "Dolcezza, I have a few calls to make. I'll be in the office. Do you need anything?"

"I'm good. I think I'm going to go and lie back down for a while." I'm still tired, and after eating all that food, I just want to sleep it off.

"What's wrong?" He looks me over from head to toe, like he's going to be able to see something no one else does.

"Nothing's wrong. I'm just tired. I promise I'm fine."

"Okay. Call if you need anything." He kisses me

gently, lingering a moment longer as he silently observes me, before exiting the room while summoning Neo and his Uncle Gabe to follow.

I wake up and grab my phone off the bedside table. It's eleven a.m. I've been asleep for three hours. I thought I'd just come and lie down for a few minutes. I mentally check in with my body. I don't feel nauseous, so that's a plus. When I woke up earlier today, I had to run into the bathroom. I really hope that's not going to happen every day. I absolutely hate being sick. I don't really think anyone likes it, but I can't stand it.

I drag myself out of bed and jump in the shower, deciding to ensure I'm a little more presentable, even if I'm not going anywhere. I find another tight bodycon dress in the closet; this one is emerald green. I wonder how much longer I'll be able to fit into these little outfits. I'm going to make the most of wearing them while I still can.

Walking downstairs, I head to the kitchen. Surely there's a little coffee hidden somewhere in this house, a stash Theo hasn't gotten to yet. I read up about drinking coffee while pregnant. I don't have to cut it out altogether. My husband is being ridiculous.

"Mrs. Valentino, can I get you anything?" A young girl wearing a maid's uniform asks.

"Uh, I'm just looking for coffee?" I question.

"Oh, we don't have any. Mr. Valentino had us throw it all out," she says.

"Well, Mr. Valentino is an ass," I grumble, opening the fridge. I'm going to have to settle for juice.

I turn back around to the girl and her wide eyes. "Oh, he's a very good boss, ma'am. I wouldn't be here if it wasn't for him."

"What do you mean?"

"Well, he saved me. Gave me a job." She shrugs and goes back to wiping down the counter.

"What did he save you from?"

"I was going through a rough spot. I was homeless. I saw... well, Mr. Valentino found me and brought me here—offered me a job, a room. He's a good man."

I smile. "He is a good man. He'd be better if he didn't throw out all the bloody coffee." I take my glass of juice with me in search of the man himself. He's not exactly hard to find. I follow the yelling and cursing coming from down the hall, which leads me straight to his office. I have no idea what they're yelling about because, of course, they're yelling in rapid-fast Italian. I do pick up the many expletives that are spilling out though.

There're no beefy guards standing at the door today—and it's wide open. All three men pause midargument and stare at me the moment I step over the threshold. "Don't stop on my account. It's not like I can understand what you're all shouting about anyway." I smirk, leaning against the wall.

"Dolcezza, how are you feeling?" T walks up and kisses my forehead. I sink into him. I don't know what it is about such a simple gesture, but that one light touch makes me feel cherished.

"I'm fine. I didn't mean to sleep so long," I say as I watch my husband drop to his knees in front of me. "Ah, T, not really the time or place," I hiss at him.

He looks up at me and smirks before kissing my midsection. "Ciao, mia bella piccola. Non vedo l'ora di incontrarti."

He rises back to his full height, and I'm left speechless. He's talking to my stomach. I wonder if the baby can hear us yet. "What did you say?"

"I said: Hello, my beautiful baby. I can't fucking wait to meet you." His smile reaches his eyes. He really is over the moon about this baby. I'm not saying I'm not happy. I'm still shocked. I'm still questioning if it's too soon, and if I'm capable of being a mother. But T's enthusiasm is so bloody cute. I can't wait to see him holding our child. I picture the man I love with a baby against his bare chest. Yes, that is a sight I really want to see.

"You know, if the baby can hear you, you should probably stop swearing. I won't have my child's first word being a curse word."

"*Our*," T says. I can't help but give him a blank stare. I swear he confuses the shit out of me sometimes. "It's not your child, Holly. It's our child."

"Oh my God! You know, you can be infuriating sometimes. Okay, I will not have *our* child's first word be a curse word. That goes for you too." I point to Neo.

"Sure, whatever you say, boss." Neo pours three glasses of whiskey from the bar. He hands one to his dad, who always seems to be the quiet observer, then brings one of the glasses over to T.

"Drink it for me. I can't drink for nine months," T says, refusing the offer.

"Why the fuck not?" Neo grunts.

"We're pregnant, and alcohol and fetuses don't mix well together."

"She's pregnant, not you. That's not how pregnancy works, moron," Gabe grunts.

"Well, if Holly has to go without for nine months, for the sake of our baby, then I'm not letting her do it alone. We're in this together, every step of the way."

"Yeah, okay, remind me of that when it comes time to push the kid out." Neo downs T's glass of whiskey in one go. "Well, this has been great and all. But you know: things to do, people to extort and all that."

"This conversation isn't over, Neo." Theo's tone is unforgiving. I'm taken aback because I've never heard him talk to his cousin like that before.

"Sure, boss, whatever you say." Neo walks out the door with a salute.

"Why do I feel like I interrupted something important?" I ask.

"You didn't. How about we go get some lunch?"

"Nope, I'm not hungry. What's going on? What are you all so uptight about right now?"

"Nothing you need to worry about, dolcezza." T tries to placate me.

"Yeah, that might have worked with your previous girlfriends, but it's not going to fly with me. Try again."

At this, Gabe laughs but tries to cover it with a cough. "Theo never had a girl before you, Holly. Well, we all thought he had Lana, but you know how that panned out. Maybe you *should* tell her, T. We're not living in the '50s. We can't expect women to just take our word for gospel. The best way to help keep them safe is to give them information. How can she keep an eye out for monsters if she doesn't know they're out there?"

T is pensive. I can tell he's considering the advice his uncle gave him. "We'll talk... over lunch. Come on, you need to eat."

"I just ate, Theo," I argue.

"Breakfast was hours ago. You're growing a human, Holly. You need food."

I roll my eyes. I think my body is plenty capable of knowing what it needs. And right now, I'm hungry for answers, not food.

Chapter Nineteen

To say I'm fucking stressed the fuck out would be the ultimate understatement. I'm putting on my best fucking poker face for the world, trying to come across like I've got everything handled. Like I know exactly what I'm doing, just waiting for the right time to move the next piece on the chess board that is fucking mafia life. Except, I don't. And I'm not.

I have no fucking clue what that Irish fucker is up

to. I thought eradicating the other Dons would be the end of it. I knew I'd get backlash from their families, from the ones stupid enough to try to move against me. What I wasn't expecting was the fucking Clover turning up on my streets. Word is he's a fucking ghost —and I don't miss the irony. People know he's here but no one seems to have actually seen him or know where the fuck he is.

I have a whole fucking family I'm supposed to be protecting, looking out for. And the only one who really fucking matters to me right now is my wife. Her safety is my first priority. I wonder if she'll consider going back to Sydney for a few weeks. But I quickly nix that idea at the thought of spending even one night without her. *Fuck going through that torture again.* I'd rather have my nails ripped out with a rusty pair of pliers.

I watch Holly picking at her food and consider if I should call the doc in to check her over. I thought pregnant chicks were supposed to eat a lot. Have cravings and all that. Why the fuck isn't she eating? "Are you feeling okay?" I ask.

"I'm fine. How about you?"

"I'd be better if you ate your food instead of just moving it around the plate."

"And I'd be better if you actually told me what was bothering you so much. I know it's not my eating habits. Is it the baby? Has it finally sunk in? Do you— have you changed your mind about it?"

"Fuck no, nothing makes me happier than the

thought of you knocked up with my kid, Holly. I fucking love the shit out of that baby already."

"Then what's wrong?"

I don't know how to give her the answers she wants. I can't burden her with everything that's going on in the streets right now.

"Just talk to me, T. Who knows, maybe I can help? Maybe you'll feel better just talking it over."

I sigh and run a hand through my hair, pulling at the ends. I can feel the thread I'm hanging by wearing thin. My breaking point is not something I want Holly to see ever again. She saw the destruction I caused when my father died. No, he didn't die; he was fucking murdered. Fucking Lana, I really fucking want to hate her so I can kill her. Is my old man rolling over in his grave with the knowledge I haven't avenged him? I laugh at the thought.

"I don't know what you want me to tell you, Holly?"

"Everything. Anything. Just talk to me, T. You are not in this alone anymore. We're a team, remember? United."

"You want to know how I have no fucking idea how I'm going to get this family through the war that's fucking brewing in the streets right now? I have men dying as we speak, dolcezza, good fucking men. Dying because of me, because of their fucking loyalty to this family. The fucking Irish have a contract on my head. Is that what you want to know?" I yell as I swipe the contents of the dining table to the floor.

It's not until I've flipped my chair back and I'm pacing the room that what I've just done sinks in. Fuck! I look at Holly, who hasn't moved an inch. To her credit, my wife doesn't cower. She doesn't jump. She just waits. Watches.

"I'm sorry. Fuck! Dolcezza, I'm sorry... I didn't... I shouldn't have yelled at you." I pick up my chair and sink back down into the seat. Resting my forearms on my legs, I let my head hang low. *I just need to breathe*, I tell myself as I silently count to ten inside my head. I need to get my shit together.

I look up. Holly still hasn't said a word. She continues to observe me, until she slowly stands and walks around the table, avoiding the mess that now covers the ground. Pushing my shoulders back, she pulls her hem up to her hips before she straddles me. Where the fuck does she keep finding these tight little dresses anyway? I run my hands down her arms, and she shivers. Holly cups my cheeks. "You can yell at me. You can throw shit around the room. I don't care. I'll still be here, always. I want to help. But I can't help if you don't let me in, T."

"Right now, I want to forget. I want to forget that my father was murdered. I want to forget that I'm the fucking head of the family and supposed to have all the answers. I want to forget that my mother hid the identity of my biological father my whole life. I just want to forget," I admit.

Holly's lips tilt up. She slides her hands down to

my waist and unfastens my belt. "I can help you forget for a little while."

"Uh-huh, and how do you plan to do that?" I ask, watching as she pulls out my cock and starts stroking.

"Mmm, I have a few ideas." She slides off my lap and down to her knees in front of me.

Her tongue glides up the seam of my tip and circles around. I groan. Then I remember what happened last time she was in this position. "Dolcezza, you don't have to do this. I don't want you getting sick."

"Shut up, T." She closes her mouth around me, sucking me right into the back of her throat.

"Oh, fuck." One of my hands rakes through her hair and tugs upward. I need to see her face. Our eyes connect and that's when I forget. In that moment, I lose myself in her, in the sensation of her wet, warm mouth sucking me, her eyes shining with unshed tears and something else. They're shining with love. Complete adoration.

"Mmm, I think I just discovered what my first pregnancy craving is going to be," she says as she drags her tongue from my balls to my tip and back down again. She closes her mouth around my balls and pumps my cock with her tight palm.

Holy shit, that feels good. "Fuck, dolcezza, what kind of fuckery are you doing down there? Don't stop. Shit!"

She looks up at me, and her lips tilt as much as they can when her mouth is full. My head falls back. I'm going to fucking come if she keeps this up. I'm not letting that happen. I gently pull on the hair still clenched in my fist and yank her up and onto my lap. My mouth slams down onto hers, our tongues dueling for ownership before she sinks into me and lets me control her movements. She doesn't know just how submissive her body is to mine.

I pull her panties to the side and dip my finger inside her, testing her readiness for me. She's fucking drenched. Her moans are like a lullaby to my ears. She pushes forward on her tippy-toes and grabs my cock, lining it up at her entrance before she slowly sinks down on me.

"Fuck me," I growl. I don't think I'll ever stop being amazed at how fucking good her pussy feels wrapped around my cock. It's fucking pure ecstasy.

Holly grinds down on me. "Oh, I fully plan to," she says as she pushes herself back up and drops down again.

"Fuck... Again. Do that again." My hands go to her hips, guiding her up slowly before slamming her back down. Fast. "I need to fuck you, Holly. I need to...." My thoughts trail off as she repeats the motion.

"Yes, T, please."

"Please what, dolcezza?" I want to hear her say it. I love hearing her say it.

"Fuck me, T. Fuck me so I can still feel you when I'm walking around tomorrow. Fuck me like you own me."

I pick her up and walk to the dining table, laying her on top of it. "I do fucking own you, dolcezza," I say as I thrust into her. I hold her hips in place as I drive forward and back. Hard and fast. "Pull your tits out. I want to see them bounce as I fuck you!" I command. She doesn't disappoint. She drags the fabric of her dress down—she's not wearing a fucking bra. I watch her tits bounce as I lose myself in her. "Best. Fucking. Pussy. Ever!" I grunt.

"Oh God, I'm..." Her mouth parts in a not-so-silent pout. And I follow her off that cliff as her screams echo against the walls.

Covered in sweat and panting, I tug her to her feet, drop her dress back in place and readjust her neckline. Then, I do up my fly and button my pants before picking her up and walking out of the room.

"What are you doing?"

"If you think I'm even remotely close to being finished with you, you're out of your beautiful fucking mind. This is far from over."

Holly's asleep on my chest. I think I literally fucked her into slumber. She crashed after the fifth orgasm I drew out of her. I make a mental note to call Doc and find out just how much her body can take in her condition. Fuck, I probably shouldn't have been as rough as I was with her; she offered me a piece of heaven, an escape, and I fucking took it with everything I had.

My phone's been vibrating for the last ten minutes. I've been ignoring it. I know if it were anything too urgent, I'd have Neo knocking on my door. Neo... Fuck. I bet he's gone and done what I warned him not to fucking do. I told him to stay under the radar, not go out looking for a fucking bullet between the eyes. I should have known better than to let him out of my sight.

I slide Holly off my body and place her head on the pillows next to me. I reach over and dig through the pockets of my pants, and find my phone before scrolling through my messages.

Fuck! I get up and quickly jump in the shower prior to getting dressed again. After strapping two Glocks and two knives to my body, I throw on my jacket and walk back into the bedroom. Holly's just starting to stir. "Dolcezza, I have to go out for a bit. Stay in the house. Don't go outside, okay?"

She jolts upright, and I'm struck dumb at the sight of her naked breasts. "T, where are you going?" she asks.

"Ah, just out. Stay inside the house," I repeat before leaning down to kiss her forehead.

Her hands cling to the lapels of my jacket. "Please stay. Don't go. T, just stay, please. Let someone else go."

Fuck me, her pleas pierce straight through my heart. I wish I could do what she's asking of me. But I can't. "Dolcezza, I can't send anyone else. I'll be fine. I'll be back before you know it."

"I can't live in a world where you don't exist, T.

Don't make me have to endure that. Promise me that you'll be back."

"Tornerò sempre da te. Ti voglio bene. Always."

"I love you too."

I pry her hands off me and walk out the door, willing myself not to look back. Because if I do, I might just cave and give her what she wants.

Chapter Twenty

Holly

He left hours ago. He should be back by now, right? Surely, whatever it is that called him away from me wasn't that bad. I have to believe that it wasn't that bad. I'm going out of my bloody mind with worry. I place a hand on my stomach and inhale deeply. My anxiety cannot be good for this little pea-sized baby. I'm no expert, but I'm pretty sure you're not meant to experience too much stress during pregnancy.

I need to calm my nerves. Usually, I'd pour myself a shot of tequila or a glass of wine, but I can't do that right now. I can't do anything other than wander around this huge museum of a house… and wait.

Wait for Theo to walk through the front door. Wait for the demons to step out of the shadows. Wait for someone to tell me my husband isn't coming back.

Theo has a contract on his head. I don't think he meant to let that bit of information slip out during his breakdown earlier, but he did. And I can't help but think someone has cashed in on that contract. I can't lose him. I won't lose him. I want to call him. Text him. *Something*. I just need a goddamn sign that he's coming home to me. I stop pacing outside T's office and turn the handle; the door opens and I step inside. Flicking the light on, I walk along the bookshelf, inspecting the piles of books on display.

I know T said this was his dad's office. All of this stuff must have belonged to Mr. Valentino. I imagine it's hard for him to be here, to be the one sitting behind the desk. I know he always knew he'd take over as head of the family, but he never thought it would be this early.

I pick up a photo of a very young Theo with his parents. They seem happy. Normal. His dad is looking down at him, smiling. There're photos of T, alone, at all stages of his life. You can tell his dad was proud of him. He was very much a loved son. That's evident in these frames. I wonder if Theo knew just how much he meant to his dad?

I pause on an image of T, Neo, and Lana as teenagers. Have they heard from her? I have her number in my phone. Maybe I should give her a call... see if she's okay. I go and curl up on the couch, pulling the throw blanket over me. Then I let the tears fall. I'm not angry that T left. He's just gone to work. That's all it is. But if I'm honest, I am scared.

Scared that this is the future I have to look forward to. Will I have to explain to our child why daddy isn't home for dinner? Will I have to hide the fact that I'm worried? Anxious?

I'll do whatever I have to do. The alternative, leaving New York and going back to Sydney without T, that's not the life I want. I swipe at the tears on my cheeks and sit up. I need to shake myself out of this. I need to stop sulking and start acting. I can do this. When T comes home, I don't want him finding me upset. That will only place more burden on his shoulders. I'm going to get better at being the wife he needs, the support he deserves. He does everything for me. He's always trying to make sure I don't want or need for anything. I have to start doing that for him.

I sit at his desk and open the laptop. The predictable password box pops up. I've seen T enter a combination of numbers before. I've just never really paid attention to what they were. I try: 1410. The date we signed our marriage papers, since it worked the last time on the burner phone. It's not that. I type in the next significant date I can think of, before finally entering in yesterday's date. The day we found out we were pregnant. Bingo, the screen comes to life. He must have changed it almost immediately after finding out.

We have three days left until we get the keys to the house I chose. I'm still in shock that T just bought the property. He didn't even look at the whole estate. He said if that's the house I wanted, then that's all that mattered. I want to make it more than a house though. I want it to be a home. Our home. I want to fill the walls with laughter, fun, love, and happiness. I want our children to always have a home they can come back to.

Like this house is for T. Like my parents' house is for me. I know I could always go home, and my mum and dad would welcome me with open arms. I know that my old bedroom will look exactly the same as it did when I left.

I do a Google search for furniture stores in New York. I don't know where to even start. The apartment was one thing, but that house is so big I wonder how we will ever completely furnish it. I know I shouldn't... but I search through T's emails for the documents from the sale. They were easy enough to find. I open the attachment with the floor plan. I'm going to just go room by room. I start with the master bedroom. That is where we seem to spend most of our time, so I want to pick out our bedroom furniture first, and then I'll move on to the rest of the house.

I startle at the noise coming from the foyer. I don't know how long I've been sitting here, getting lost in the online shopping portal, but I've just ordered furniture for our bedroom, one living room, a dining table, and a heap of kitchen appliances and utensils. I kept waiting for Theo's fancy black cards to decline. It became more of a game: how much can I spend before it tells me it's too much? I didn't cheap out either, already raking up several hundred grand for just a few rooms. I wonder what Theo will think about the items I've purchased.

I know he's back. If the voices carrying through the house didn't tell me, that sense of calm that rushed over me a moment ago would have. I should go and see what all the chaos is about. But before I can get up, the door pushes open and T walks in with Neo right behind him. They both stop when they see me at the computer.

Neither of them says a word, but Neo makes a point of shutting and locking the door, before he smirks. "You know, I never realized just how fucking hot it would be to have a female boss. Too bad the family traditions are so archaic and no one's open to changing them. Because fuck, you look good sitting behind that desk, Holly."

"You've clearly lost your fucking mind, Neo. I

should probably get you committed, because that's the only reason I can think of that you'd be stupid enough to hit on my fucking wife," T growls at him. Yes, growls —that deep, rough, commanding growl that goes straight to my core every time. My eyes never waiver from him as he silently walks behind me to peer over my shoulder. "You're furniture shopping?" he asks, surprise evident in his tone.

"A little. I figured we're probably going to need something... you know, to sleep on, sit on, eat in."

"Fuck on." Neo laughs. I pick up a pencil from the desk and toss it at him; he dodges it easily.

"Next time throw the paperweight, dolcezza. Did anyone see you sitting in here?" T asks.

"Um, I don't think so, why?"

"Wait, don't answer that yet. Let me fetch some popcorn first," Neo says, heading for the door.

"Fuck off, Neo. Don't think we've finished that conversation either."

I look between the cousins. There's a tension that isn't usually there. "Ah, I can go, you know, if you've got shit to do. I was just about to see what's in the fridge anyway."

I stand up from the chair, ready to exit the room. There's a bit too much alpha male assholeness filling the air in here—too much for my liking. T grabs me around the waist, pulling my back against his chest. His hand rests on my stomach, and his thumb rubs up and down in little twirls. "You're staying. He's leaving."

"Right, catch you later. Holly, be gentle. He didn't

come up with the rules." Neo's parting words confuse me.

I turn around to face T, before reaching up and melting my lips against his. "Mmm, I missed you."

"I fucking miss you every second that goes by where I'm not touching you." He picks me up and sits me on the desk. He lowers himself down in his chair and stares at me, as if trying to read my expression.

It's obvious he wants to say something. "Just say it already. Whatever it is, it can't be that bad."

"Okay, but just know I didn't make the rules and I don't always agree with them. But I do have to uphold them. Mostly."

"T, spit it out. What happened?" I'm getting worried he's going to tell me something really bad. Like we're not actually married. Oh my God, is that a possibility?

"You can't sit in this chair. You shouldn't even be in the office without me in here. But you absolutely cannot sit at this desk."

I can't sit at his desk? I blink in response. Once, then twice. I pinch my arm. Nope, not dreaming this shit. I burst out in hysterics.

"I'm serious, Holly. You can't be seen sitting here."

"Oh, I know you are. That's why it's so bloody funny. Geez, T, I thought you were going to give me some really bad news or something. So you don't want me in your office? Fine. I won't come in here alone."

"It's not that I don't want you in here, or that I don't trust you, Holly. It's just the rules. No one is to sit in the boss's seat. Anyone who thought to do so would have a bullet between their eyes, because it's an outright challenge for the throne."

"But I'm your wife. I'm hardly going to challenge you for your *throne*." I use air quotes because it's bloody ridiculous.

"I know that, but others... they don't. I just... For your own safety and to prevent gossip amongst the family, just choose any other seat."

"Okay. Now can we go get some food?"

"Yes. Thank you for understanding. Also, hello in there, little guy. Did you keep your mama company while I was out?" T lifts my shirt and kisses my bare stomach.

"Your credit cards kept me company while you were out."

"Our. They're our cards, dolcezza. It's not my money. It's our money."

"Okay, well, *our* money is now short a few hundred grand," I admit, looking into his eyes as I wait for his reaction. "I may have gone a little overboard on the whole luxury furniture thing."

"Holly, we just paid thirty-five million dollars for a home. Did you really think we were going to fill it with furniture from Goodwill?"

"Well, no, I guess not. But I want to donate all the stuff in my apartment to Goodwill or somewhere. I don't need it."

"That's a great idea. We'll donate the stuff in the penthouse too."

"You don't want to keep the penthouse?" I ask.

"Nope, we'll find another one. One that's not tainted with bad memories." Bad memories like two people being murdered there and posed to look like us. Yeah, I certainly wouldn't be in a hurry to go back there anytime soon. "Come on, let's get you two some food."

I can't help but smile and roll my eyes at him. I'm not just *me* anymore.

Chapter Twenty-One

Walking into the kitchen, I did not expect to be greeted by the scene that's in front of me. "What the fuck?" I reach behind me to grab for my Glock, but Holly seems to have developed superhuman reflexes and beats me to it.

"I'm not letting you shoot him," she hisses at me. I smirk. She doesn't know that not only do I have more guns on me right now, but I don't need a weapon to kill the bastard. I've never wanted to fucking wring his neck with my bare hands so badly before.

"Ah, T, it's not what it looks like," Neo stammers.

"Really, because what it looks like is that you just had your slimy little tongue down my sister's fucking throat."

"Well, fuck, I guess it is what it looks like." He smirks, his hands lifted in surrender.

"Seriously, you just couldn't fucking help yourself?" I yell. "And you." I point at Angelica. "You can do way better than the likes of him."

"Thanks, I love you too, coz."

"Okay, settle down, Theo. I've managed my whole life without a sibling. I don't need you doing the whole big brother act now. He's hot. I was bored, so I kissed him. If it makes you feel any better, it was my doing, not his." Angelica places herself in front of Neo, which I find odd.

"Yeah, and I bet he put up a real fucking fight." Shit, I need to do something. I need to calm down somehow.

"Ah, T, I want a cheeseburger. Can we go get burgers?" Holly asks.

I look directly at her stomach, cursing myself for forgetting she was hungry. But she's out of her fucking mind if she thinks I'm going to be feeding our kid that crap. "No. You're not eating fucking fast-food burgers. If you want a burger, I'll make you one." Opening the freezer, I start pulling down ingredients. Out of the corner of my eye, I see Holly sit on the counter stool.

"Do you want me to help? I can get some salads?" she half-heartedly offers.

"Nope, you just sit, dolcezza. I've got this."

"Any chance I can get one of those burgers?" Neo asks, sitting next to my wife. I glare at him without answering. "I'll take that as a no. Holly, it was a pleasure to see you as always. Angelica, well, thanks for sharing saliva. I'm sure I'll see you around. You know where to find me, T." He walks out, and I hear the front door of the house slam shut a few minutes later.

Holly jumps to her feet and is headed to the doorway when I intercept. I don't know why the idea of her walking out makes me fucking panic so damn much. "Where are you going?"

"To the bathroom, just down the hall. I'll be right back." Pushing up on her tiptoes, she kisses my lips lightly. I watch as she sashays down the hall and into the bathroom.

I turn around and am greeted by Angelica's stone-cold stare. "Really, Theo? I don't need you butting into my life like that."

"No, you probably don't. But as long as you're my sister, you'll just have to get used to it."

She tilts her head to the side. "I know thirty different ways to kill you and make it look like an accident."

"I know fifty." I shrug.

"Argh, are you always this infuriating?"

"Probably."

"I think I actually like him, you know. Am I not

good enough for your friend? Is it because I have a kid? Because I come with baggage? What is it?"

"No, it's because he's not good enough for you. For Isabella," I tell her.

"Why? What makes him so bad? And if he really is that awful, why is he here so freely? Walking through *your* house, hanging around *your* wife, your family?"

Well, shit, she has me there. I can't fucking think of a reason why Neo isn't good enough. He's the best fucking guy I know. "I don't know. He's a good man, loyal as fuck, and I know he'd lay down his life for anyone in this family. But really, Angelica? Could you not just go find yourself some accountant or something?"

"Yeah, I could see that going down real well when it came time to meet the families." She laughs.

"I don't want to see you get hurt. And I don't want to have to shoot my best friend because he's the one who hurt you."

"Why do you think he'd hurt me?"

"I've never known Neo to have a steady girl. He's never been interested in relationships. He can also be a little... unpredictable. He's a made man, Angelica. And I have my niece to consider."

"So, he's like you? Like Papa?"

"Yes."

"Well, I may not know you very well yet. But I've seen how you treat Holly, and I've seen how you treat women in general. And I know my dad would never hurt a woman on purpose. I don't consider that a bad trait in a partner."

I look into her eyes and I see it. She has true feelings for Neo. This wasn't *just because she was bored.* "This wasn't the first time, was it?"

"No."

"When? How many times?"

"It doesn't matter. What matters is I need you to not make this difficult for me."

"Fucking hell, why? Seriously, what the fuck have I done wrong in my life for this to happen?"

"Did you ever think that this actually has nothing to do with you? Whatever Neo and I choose to do, or not do, is on us. Not you."

Holly walks back into the room. "I agree. You need to leave them alone, Theo."

"You're supposed to be on my side here, dolcezza."

"I am. Always. Which is why I'm telling you that, unless you want to lose them both, you need to stay out of it. You can't control everyone, T."

"Well fuck, Holly, why do you have to be right all the fucking time?"

"Because I'm always right?" she questions.

"Mmm, sure. Sit down. These burgers won't take long." Then I turn to Angelica. "Where's Isabella?"

"She's with Papa. He took her out riding somewhere."

"Riding what?" I ask.

"Ponies."

I roll my eyes. Of course he bribes her with fucking

ponies. I make a mental note to add a stable to our new house.

I left Holly in the movie room with Angelica, promising I wouldn't be out long. I shouldn't be surprised that he's in the first place I look for him. The fucking basement. "Took you long enough. I was starting to think you weren't going to show." Neo rises up from the ground, dusting his pants off.

"I had more pressing matters to deal with first. Thought I'd leave you to stew in the shit you've gone and gotten yourself into for a bit." I undo the buttons of my shirt and hang it on a hook on the cement wall. I unstrap the knives on my ankles and throw them to the ground. I made a point of leaving my guns upstairs. I don't want to be tempted to actually kill the fucker. Just make him bleed.

"So, how's this going to go? Am I supposed to hold back now that you're the Don?"

"If you hold back, I'll fucking kill you, Neo. You give as good as you get. If you can."

He nods once. We've been sparring all our lives. It's a fair match—that's for sure. But I've got something he hasn't right now. Burning fucking rage. Because of the fucking war that's going on. Because I'm in a position I wasn't fucking ready for. Because I can't fucking find the Irish fucking Clover. And because my best friend went and fucked around with my sister. With that thought, I swing. Hard. Fast. He doesn't see it coming, and it knocks him back a step.

"That was a cheap shot," he says, shaking his head.

"How many times?" I ask, swinging again and connecting with his lower ribs.

"You'll have to be more specific." He lands a left hook on my jaw.

"Fucker, how many fucking times have you touched my sister?"

"She's only been your sister for a few days."

"How many fucking times?" We throw punch for punch. My knuckle cuts his lower lip, and I smirk. I was first to draw blood. And just like this war, I'll make sure I'm the last too.

"Three times. You want specific details? Because that's fucking messed up, even for you."

"Fuck you. I told you not to touch her."

"Yeah, well, I guess I didn't hear you."

I swing my leg behind him and kick his knees out from under him. I launch myself forward and start laying into him everywhere I can connect flesh to flesh. He blocks most of my blows but not all. "Start fucking listening."

"If you want me to stop seeing her, you'll have to fucking kill me. If you make me choose, T, I will fucking choose her. Over you. Over anyone." He manages to roll me to my back and lands a hit to my right eye.

"Fuck you." I jerk him off me and jump to my feet. "You've known her for a few days; you can't be in love with her."

He drops his arms, and his face goes ashen white, like he's seen the ghost of the last man he buried. "You're right. I can't be. Can I? What the fuck did you do to me?"

"Me? I didn't fucking do shit."

"I was fine, until your love sickness or some shit passed on to me. This is your fault," he yells, pulling at his hair. "I'm not ready for this shit, man."

"Well, you better fucking get ready, because my sister doesn't need a fucking pussy. She needs someone man enough to go after what he wants. Someone who won't fucking back down. So, man the fuck up, Neo. Or get the fuck out."

"You don't even want me with her anyway."

"Yeah, well, apparently, I don't actually get to choose that. She wants you, so you better not fucking disappoint her."

"She said that?"

"What are we? Fucking middle school cheer-leaders?"

"Right. You good?" he asks, looking me up and down.

"Fine, you?"

"Fine."

I pick up my shirt and we walk up the stairs together. "You do know she's a package deal, right? It's not just her; it's Isabella too."

"I know," he says.

I was hoping Holly and Angelica would still be in the movie room when we came back up. But both women are standing in the middle of the foyer. Holly, with a shocked expression. And Angelica, pissed off. Neo knew he'd have to face the consequence for disobeying my direct order. If it were anyone else, they'd have their fucking hands ripped off. My sister starts cursing at us both in a string of Italian.

"Relax. He's still in one piece," I say, walking up to Holly. "Come on, I need a shower."

"You look like you need a doctor. Both of you." She glances from me to Neo, and back to me again. "Why would you do this?"

"This is nothing, dolcezza. I'm okay."

"No, you're not. Come on." I let Holly take my hand and pull me in the direction of our bedroom.

Chapter Twenty-Two

I can't believe they would fight like that. They look like they just went ten rounds with bloody Mike Tyson. I'm furious at them both. I don't understand the need to beat each other to a pulp. What would that even solve?

"Dolcezza, I'm fine," T says as I shove him into the bathroom.

"Zip it. I don't want to hear it, T. You're fine. Really? Have a look in the mirror. Look at your face and tell me again that you're fine." Opening the cabinets, I find a first aid kit at the back. I get to work pulling out antibacterial ointment and wipes.

"Holly, this is nothing. It will heal."

"You have a swollen eye, and there's blood running down your face. Not to mention, the rest of the bruises I can see developing all over you. Really? How would you feel if I came home to you like this?"

"The world would be in trouble because I'd go on a fucking rampage."

"Exactly. Do you have any idea how much I wanted to fucking hurt Neo just now?"

"Well, I think I may have gotten one or two good hits in."

"Argh, you're so infuriating."

"Not the first time I've heard that."

"Sit still and let me clean you up."

T wraps his arms around me. Even though he's covered in sweat and blood, I let myself take comfort in his embrace. "I'm sorry. I don't want you to worry, dolcezza."

"You're hanging on by a thread, T. What if you had lost it when you were fighting with Neo? What if you snapped? You'd never forgive yourself."

"I wouldn't have let things get that far. This isn't the first time Neo and I have sparred. And I'd be lying if I said it'll be the last."

"I don't like seeing you hurt."

"I know. But I'm okay. I promise. Not even a broken rib, dolcezza. I'll mend in no time."

After showering, Theo and I lie in bed and decide on a rom-com to watch. Halfway through the movie, I feel sleep taking over. "T, where did you disappear to today? What'd you have to do?"

His whole body stiffens beneath me, causing me to look up. I drop my head back on his chest and wait him out—to see if he'll shut down or open up to me. After a few minutes, he sighs. "Neo found someone we were looking for. He had him in the warehouse. I had to go and see if I could get answers out of him."

"And did you? Get answers?"

"Not enough. But some."

"Want to tell me about it? I might be able to help, you know."

"There's a guy. He goes by the name: The Clover. He's Irish, obviously. He's the fucker with the contract on my head. It seems I've caused a bit of havoc in the operation he was running here in New York."

"What kind of operation?"

"The child sex ring I went to Italy to stop. They were importing stolen girls and selling them right here, under our noses. Between me and Lana's uncle, we've intercepted three of their shipments and saved those girls. They're not exactly happy about that."

"What kind of monsters are selling little girls? That makes me sick."

"Yeah, it's fucked up. I'm not about to let them do that in my city."

"I'm glad. So how do we kill this Clover guy?"

T's chest shakes with laughter. "Dolcezza, *we* don't do anything. As soon as I find him, I will kill him. Trust me."

"What if he finds you first, T? We're about to have a child. I can't do this alone."

"You won't have to. Our son or daughter will have both of us, Holly."

"Which one do you want?"

"Huh?"

"A son or daughter? Which one do you want the most?"

"In my position, I'm supposed to say a son. Someone to take over the family business—*if* he wants to. But, honestly, I'd fucking love a daughter. A mini you? I couldn't think of anything better. What about you?"

"I don't know. I just want a healthy baby. And I want to be the kind of mother my mum was growing up. She was always there for us. Would drop whatever she was doing for me and Reilly. I'm worried that I don't really have it in me to do this. I'm scared I won't love this child like it deserves to be loved, T." I don't know why I can't stop these thoughts from coming up. I need to get my head in the game. This baby is happening. I'm going to be someone's mother. I have to start thinking like it.

"Dolcezza, you are going to love this child more than you could ever love me. I know you will."

"I don't think that's possible, T. I love you so freaking much. I can't think of anyone I'd put above you. Don't you dare ever tell Reilly that, or I will kill you myself."

"You know, I thought I had loved people before. My parents. Neo *sometimes*. But you, Holly, it's a different kind of love. It's something I've never experienced. And this baby, that's a different kind of love too. I can't wait to meet him, or her. I'm jealous as fuck that you get to carry it around inside you, and I can't. I know that you will love this child. It won't be the same way that you love me, and that's okay. It will be more powerful, Holly, trust me."

"You're jealous of not being the one who's going to get fat? That's odd."

"Well, I can let myself go. Get a big beer gut or something if you want?" he offers.

"Nope, I'm good with just how you are now." I run my hands down his naked chest, over the ridges of his abs and back up again. "You know, if this Clover guy is Irish, have you tried looking in plain sight? Around the Irish community?"

"We've got people scouring the city for him, Holly. We will find him."

"Maybe there's a way to draw him out?"

"Maybe, I really don't want you to worry about it though. I've got this handled."

"I thought we were a team now? United and all that."

"We are, but you need to sleep. I have a surprise for you arriving tomorrow night. You'll want to be well rested."

"A surprise? What is it?"

"If I told you, it wouldn't be a surprise. Go to sleep, dolcezza. I love you."

"Argh, I hate surprises," I groan.

"No, you don't."

I've been on pins and needles all day. T went to the office for a few hours and then came back cool as a cucumber. I've tried to get him to tell me what the surprise is, but he won't budge.

It's past dinnertime, and I'm starting to think that there isn't actually a surprise at all. But that's okay. Because right now, curled up in the movie room with my husband, I have everything I could ever need.

"You guys do know it's only eight o'clock at night, and you're in New York fucking City—the city that doesn't sleep. Why the hell are you in pjs watching TV? Are you fifty already?"

I jump (like literally jump) off the couch the moment I hear the voice. By the time she's finished her little lecture, I've tackled her and she stumbles back a couple of steps. "What? How? Why?" I can't seem to get my thoughts out.

Reilly is here, right in front of me. "Well, I bloody missed you too, sis."

"I can't believe you're here. And we're not in bloody pjs," I squeal. Yep, I focus on that part of her speech.

"Well, you can thank your hunky hubby for that. He sent a jet and practically ordered me to get on it. And that dress? *Damn*, Hol. Def not pjs. I'm so glad we're the same size. I'm stealing all of your clothes before I leave."

"Correction: I asked, nicely. And did you really just say you're stealing shit from a mafia boss's house?" T says from behind me in his *no nonsense* tone.

"No, there was no question about it. You said: *Reilly, your sister needs you. I'm sending a car to pick you up now.*" Reilly does her best *Godfather* accent, but totally butchers it, all while ignoring the bit about stealing my clothes.

"You had the option to say no," T argues.

"Sure I did." Reilly laughs. "Have you tried saying no to this one?" She then points to me.

"Yes, I have actually."

"And how well did that end for you?"

"I've had more pleasurable waterboarding experiences," T deadpans.

Bray, who's been quiet throughout the ordeal,

comes over and hugs me. "How you holding up, Hol? I hear you went and got yourself knocked up. I'd appreciate it if the morning sickness would stop though."

"How did you know I've been sick?" I ask, confused.

"Because she has been too. We even went and took a test just to be sure."

"Oh, sorry." Though, secretly, I'm glad I'm not in this alone.

"It's fine. We can throw up together in the morning. Come on, sit down and let me talk to my nephew."

"It could be a girl, you know," I tell Reilly.

"It's not," she says firmly. Reilly likes to think she's somewhat of a clairvoyant when it comes to these sorts of things. She's not, but I'll humor her. "Hey, little guy, I'm your favorite Auntie Rye. You'll love me most because I'm just like your mummy," she whispers to my stomach, and my heart swells. I can't help the smile that stays plastered across my face.

"I've had one of the guest suites set up for you. We move into our own house in two days."

"You bought a new house? When? Where? You didn't tell me?" Reilly excitedly pulls out her phone. "What's the address? Let me look it up."

T rattles off the details to her, and she screams when it comes up on her screen. Then he leans in and kisses my cheek. "And that's my cue to leave. Bray, you want a drink?" he offers.

"Yeah, man, sure." My brother-in-law mumbles

something to Reilly, and her face reddens, before he follows Theo out the door.

"Okay, spill. What in the actual fuck, Holly? This is not a house. This is... I don't know what this is, but it's insane."

"I know. It's perfect, right?"

"It's a fucking mansion, on mansion steroids. Holly, what could you possibly need a house so big for? When we drove up to this place, I thought I was at the wrong address, then I started seeing all the goons around in black suits and figured it had to be right. Bray totally wants to go to a hotel, by the way."

"He doesn't want to stay here?"

"He doesn't think it's safe."

"This house is a fortress, Rye. It's plenty safe. Plus, there are hidden little panic rooms everywhere. I'll show you where some of them are."

"If it's such a fortress, why do you need panic rooms?"

"No idea. But they are there."

"Okay, so how about a tour? Show me around. What do you do all day here?" she asks.

"Lately, I've been online furniture shopping. Buying stuff for the new house."

"Oh, that I can help with. Spending your hubby's money is going to be my new favorite pastime."

I laugh. Of course it is.

After showing Reilly around, we find Bray and T in the game room playing pool. I haven't seen anyone use this room. But judging by the way T is scrutinizing the table and balls and how he's bent over holding the cue, yep, he's done this once or twice before. And I suddenly have an urge to jump on the table, spread myself open for him, and have him bent over my body like that. Bloody hell, how did I get this god of a man?

"Hol, do me a favor. Come and stand over here for a sec." Bray beckons me with his finger. Confused, I go and stand beside him. "Thanks, you might just be the distraction I need, so he actually misses a shot."

"Wait, you're losing?" I ask. The infamous Bray Williamson does not lose. At anything. According to him, anyway.

"I'm not losing. I'm just not winning yet."

"Well, I'm not helping you beat him," I say, gesturing towards my husband. I walk around the table and approach Theo. Leaning into his ear, I whisper, "I need you to win this game already, so you can kick these two out, lay me across this table, and fuck me."

T's lips tilt up at one corner as he looks me over. "Reilly, did Holly show you where your room is?"

"Yes, thank you," she responds.

"Good." He throws the cue down. "Bray, you win."

T leans forward, and the next minute, I'm over his shoulder. "It's been a long day. Holly's tired. Good night," he calls back as he exits the room.

I don't hear their response, but I do hear my sister's laughter. Not even a moment later, T is bounding up the stairs and slamming our bedroom door shut.

He stands me on my feet and steps back. "That dress, lose it. Now," he commands, and my panties dampen at his tone.

I reach behind me and pull the zipper down, letting the straps drop from each of my shoulders, before the material falls to the floor and I step out of it. I'm left standing in a matching black lace panty and bra set. "Lose the shirt," I tell him.

"Tsk, tsk, tsk. That's not how this works, dolcezza. You don't give the orders. You obey mine."

I want to argue that point, but more than that, I want him to tell me what to do right now. It's confusing the hell out of me.

T circles me like a predator eyeing its prey, his fingertips trailing their way up my spine. "Va tutto bene, dolcezza. Ti farò stare davvero bene." I have no idea what he just said, but God, does it sound freaking hot. "I'm going to make you feel so good," he growls, unclasping my bra. He slowly drags the straps down my arms before the lace flutters to the floor and my breasts hang heavy, my chest rising and falling with each labored breath. He cups my breasts in his hands, his fingers pinching and pulling at my nipples. I lean my head back against him. "Open your eyes. Look. I want you to see how I make you feel. I want you to see how fucking beautiful you are when you come for me." One of his hands draws my head up, and as my lashes part, my gaze immediately connects with his through the floor-to-ceiling mirror on the wall. The heat in his eyes is intoxicating. "Do you see it, Holly? Do you see how fucking gorgeous you are?"

When I look at my reflection, I take note of my flushed skin. My hair, a tumbled mass of red, hanging over my shoulder. My eyes, glassy with pleasure and need. My chest heaving, causing my breasts to push out and seek his touch. I look wanton. I look like a needy bloody woman in heat.

"Fucking sensational. You are sensational, dolcezza. And mine. All of this..." The palm of his hand runs smoothly over my still-flat stomach. "...is mine."

"Yours," I agree. Because I *am* his.

His fingers dip inside my panties, and he circles around my clit. "Do you want me to make you come on my fingers, Holly."

The way my name rolls off his tongue sends tingles straight to my core. "Y-Yes," I whimper as my knees begin to buckle. His teeth graze the side of my neck, and my whole body trembles. He thrusts two fingers inside, grinding his palm on my clit as he perfectly glides in and out of me. "Oh God!" My pelvis moves in rhythm with his hand, seeking something more. The moment he bites down on my neck, that's when I get the *more* and I completely collapse. If it weren't for T holding me upright, I'd be nothing but a mushy puddle on the floor.

"Fucking beautiful. I could watch you do that over and over again and still not get enough," he growls as he picks me up and throws me on the bed. Then he slides my panties down my legs, scrunches them up in one hand, brings them to his nose, and inhales, before tucking them in his pocket. "Spread your legs. Show me how wet *my* pussy is, Holly."

I open my thighs as wide as I possibly can.

"Good girl," he praises. "Now, put your fingers inside yourself. Keep it warm for me."

Slowly, with a shaky hand, I find my clit before sliding down farther and inserting two fingers. They don't feel anywhere as good as Theo's. But doing this. To myself. In front of him. While watching him undress... I'm getting really bloody worked up again.

"Don't you dare fucking come. You're only keeping it warm for me, dolcezza."

I groan and try to lessen my pace. But I'm really close to the edge. "T, please, I need... I need..."

"I know what you need, Holly. I've got it right here," he says, stroking his cock up and down twice. He kneels on the bed, removes my fingers, and brings them to his mouth before sucking them clean. "Mmm, best thing I've ever tasted," he groans. He positions his cock at my entrance. "I called the doc, you know."

What? Is he sick? Why the hell is he talking about the doctor now?

"I wanted to make sure that fucking you the way I like wouldn't hurt the baby."

"What?"

"It won't, by the way. Doc assures me that we can fuck as often and as much as we want."

"Well, gee, I'm glad you got that reassurance. I could have told you that, T," I sass.

He thrusts his cock to the hilt—in one, deep, hard motion—effectually taking the sass right out of my mouth. "Huh, maybe all I had to do to stop you from being so fucking mouthy with me was shove my cock into your greedy, little, tight cunt. Seems you're speechless now, dolcezza."

"You can always try," I grit out as he pistons into me again. He picks up both of my legs, resting my ankles on his shoulders. His hands lift my hips, and at this angle, he feels like he's somehow deeper inside me. Is that even possible? He starts off slow, gliding his cock in and out at an easy, torturous pace. "Harder, T, fuck me harder." I try to move my hips to meet his thrusts, but his firm grip isn't allowing me the reprieve.

"Say please, Holly. Where have your manners gone?" He smirks.

I could argue. *Be stubborn.* But that's not going to get me what I want right now. No, the quickest and easiest way to get what I want is to comply. "Please fuck me, T. I need you." He doesn't disappoint. He starts pumping in and out at a pace that literally takes my breath away. "Oh God! Yes, don't stop," I scream, not caring who the hell hears me right now.

"Never. Fuck, dolcezza. I love you, but fuck, I want to worship your fucking pussy every day. I doubt even heaven feels this fucking good."

I have no words. I'm crashing, and my body is on fire, ignited by the pleasure coursing through my every nerve ending. Everything goes quiet, and the world fades out as I let myself go. I explode into a million pieces, a beautiful rapture of my being as stars cloud my vision.

I'm vaguely aware of T's body stiffening, followed by a string of Italian expletives as he fills my pussy.

Chapter Twenty-Three

I can't believe I'm leaving Holly in bed, naked, looking so fuckable. Stroking her hair, I gently wake her. "Dolcezza, I'm heading out for a bit. Stay inside the house, okay," I whisper into her ear.

Her eyes spring open, the fear in them so evident before she tries to hide it. "How long will you be?" she asks.

"Not long. Go to sleep. I'll be back before you know it." I kiss her temple.

"Promise?"

"Promise. Tornerò sempre da te, Holly," I repeat the promise I've said many times before.

"Always," she agrees.

I lift the blanket and kiss her stomach. "Ti amo, bambino mio. Sii buono e cerca di non far ammalare troppo la mamma stamattina." I fucking hate leaving her, but I can't end this fucking war by hiding out at home. I need to go and get shit done.

"I love you," Holly says, grabbing my face and smashing her lips on mine.

"Not as much as I love you." I walk out and meet Neo in front of the house. "You ready for this?" I ask, giving him a once-over. Unlike me, he isn't sporting a fucking black eye from our fight. He does, however, still have a fat lip. Mouth injuries are the fucking worst. Give me broken bones any day over that shit. They just keep splitting open every time you try to fucking eat something.

"Yep, you good?"

"Let's just get this shit done so I can get back in bed with my wife."

"Yeah, there's someone I'd like to get back into bed with too." He smirks while eyeing up the house. I don't respond, but the glare I send him tells him everything my words don't. "Too soon?" He laughs.

"Neo, there will never be a time when I want to hear about you being in fucking bed with my sister."

"Right, got ya." He opens the driver's side door, as I head to the passenger side. We're doing this shit alone.

It's how we get shit done. We're quieter, quicker. And they don't usually see us coming. "How'd you find him?" Neo questions. I can tell he's annoyed at himself for not being the one to find the fucker.

"Something Holly said. I had a few guys go into the Irish community and ask around. Took a fair chunk of fucking cash, but they got an address. That's where we're going."

"So, we're steamrolling into fucking Irish territory, with nothing to go on but a fucking address where the Clover may or may not be?"

"Yep, got a problem with that? You can always wait at home. Go and finish painting your fucking nails or something, if you want." I glance towards his left hand with three pink nails.

"I don't care if you don't like them. Izzy wanted to paint them so I let her."

I do a double take and stare at him. Who the fuck is he? Because the Neo I know wouldn't even talk to a kid, let alone hang out and play dress-up. Believe me, Lana tried to practice on us when we were kids. She never succeeded. Maybe she needs to take lessons from Izzy.

"What's the plan anyway?"

"There isn't one. We're going to hunt this fucker down and send him back to hell."

"Great, so what if we're walking into a trap right now? Alone."

"No one knows what we're doing. How can it be a trap?"

"It's the fucking Clover. Guy's fucked up, T. Don't underestimate that level of crazy."

"We've dealt with worse." We drive the rest of the way in silence. I can tell the lack of information is killing him. He hates going into any situation blind. His hands tap relentlessly on the steering wheel. "Pull over, here. We'll walk the rest of the way. How many you got?"

"Three, four extra mags. You?"

"Four, five extra." I smirk.

Neo rolls his eyes. "Not everything is a fucking competition, coz. Just don't fucking die on me. I refuse to be the one delivering that news to your wife again."

"I'll try not to," I joke, but I have more reasons to live now than I ever have before. I have no intention of fucking dying. Neo and I wordlessly walk down the darkened path, the streetlights all busted out. Who the fuck lives in these parts? The place looks like it belongs in a third-world country, not the fucking United States of America. We get a few looks our way, and I notice some fucker pick up a phone as soon as he spots us. "We've been sighted."

Neo cracks his knuckles and stretches his arms out. "Good, it's been a while since I've had a good fight."

"I kicked your ass two nights ago, asshole. Happy to offer you a repeat if you want."

"Sure you did, if that's what you have to tell yourself to sleep at night."

"Just fucking be on—" I don't get to finish my sentence as something knocks me over the back of the head. I watch Neo slump to the ground, right before I follow suit.

The smell hits me first, then the throbbing in my temples. I go to bring my hand up to my head, to inspect for injury, but there's no fucking give. Fuck. Keeping my neck craned and my eyes closed, I can hear the distant murmurs. I do a mental check of my body: my ankles are bound, my hands are bound, and I'm sitting on something hard. Fuck, I'm tied to a fucking chair. *These fuckers tied me to a fucking chair.* My first thought is Neo. I remember seeing him go down too. I can't hear him. He's either not in the same room, or he's still out of it... or pretending to be, just like me.

"Can't we just fuck 'em up already?" someone yells.

"Boss said to keep them here, in one piece, until he gets back."

At that, I lift my head and smirk at the asshole. I don't say anything. I don't have to.

"Ah, look who's awake, the almighty Theo Valentino. Got yourself into a bit of a strife here, mate."

"I'm not you're fucking mate, cocksucker," I spit at him. I spot Neo to the left of me, his body still slumped over. His chest is moving though—*thank fucking God.* I can't do anything to prevent the blow that lands on my cheek. So I smile and embrace the pain. These fuckers can try all they want, but they'll never fucking break me. This isn't the first time I've found myself tied to a fucking chair. My fingers work at the rope around my wrists. They're fucking amateurs. I already know how I'm going to get my hands free. But I'll wait. I want their fucking boss.

"I can't wait for the boss to get here. Heard he's got a gift for us. A nice little redhead for us all to enjoy... while you watch."

My mind goes to where I left Holly, in bed. There's no way they have her. There's no way they would have gotten into that fucking house. "Sure, whatever you say." I smirk, calling their bluff. They're looking to rattle me. As much as I want to fucking kill these fuckers, all fucking three of them, I won't. I'll wait, on the off-chance that bastard has gotten his filthy fucking hands on my wife. My stomach twists at the mere thought. Noah Kelly is one sick bastard. There's no way she'll come back from that unscathed.

I look to Neo, urging the fucker to wake the fuck up. I see his right eye blink. He's awake. These three fucking idiots have grossly underestimated us. The Clover has underestimated us. To leave us tied up here, with only three fucking men. He obviously doesn't know who the fuck he's dealing with. Bring it on. I have so much fucking rage to expel, and who better to take it out on than the fucking four-leaf Clover himself. That bastard's luck is about to run dry, right as I hang him upside down and slit his shamrock-loving throat.

"He's been watching you for weeks. You think he didn't know you'd come tonight? You've got a fucking rat. Someone in your own family sold you out." One of the guys laughs.

"Yeah, well, I guess you won't mind giving me a name, considering I'm not gonna make it out of here alive anyway."

"Glad to see you know the situation you've gotten yourself into. Don't worry, I'll make sure to take real good care of that pretty wife of yours." He smirks in my face.

I laugh as I spit at him. "Good luck with that." Holly is not a weak, little, timid thing. She may look small. She may look like she can't and won't fight for herself. But I pity the fuckers if they actually do have her. If they bring her here, there will be blood spilled, and it won't be ours.

Another fist lands on my face, and I see fucking stars. Fuck me, how about a little creativity? The blows to the head are getting old and my temples fucking pound. I need to stay conscious. I need to stay alert. I can't get the fuck out of here if I let these bastards knock me out again.

"Boss is on his way up," one of the Irish fucks announces, looking at his phone.

I start the process of loosening the ropes around my wrists. I can still feel the blade at my ankle when I move my leg. Like I said, fucking amateurs. It will take me precisely ten seconds to retrieve that knife and cut myself free. Neo finally decides to make himself known. "Good, I was starting to get fucking bored listening to you assholes."

"Don't worry, you can listen to your girl's scream instead."

"Go for it. I don't have a fucking girl," Neo counters. And I chuckle and shake my head. But my laughter instantly dies off and my heart sinks when I see the fucking redheaded son of a bitch walk through the door with my wife and sister, a gun in each hand and aimed at their heads.

Chapter Twenty-Four

Holly

When T left, I tossed and turned but I couldn't get back to sleep, so I went downstairs to make a hot chocolate. I can't bring myself to drink the decaffeinated shit T is trying to pass off as coffee. I'm trying not to think about why he had to leave the house at all hours of the morning. It's only just breaking daylight outside now, and he's been gone for at least two hours. I'm pouring some milk into a pot and putting it on the stove when Angelica walks into the kitchen.

"Morning. You're up early. Are you sick again?"

"Um, no, thank God. Not yet, anyway. I'm making hot chocolate. Want one?"

"I'd much rather have some coffee, but sure, since your husband has decided to be overbearing, I'll settle for a hot chocolate."

"I'd die for one of Helena's coffee's right now," I groan.

"We should just go. You know T and Neo are not going to be back for ages. They won't even know we left."

"I don't know... Theo asked me to stay in the house." I bite my lip, the temptation for a good hot cup of coffee strong.

"Do you always do everything he orders you to do?" Angelica questions, with a raised eyebrow.

"He didn't order me; he asked. There's a difference."

"Okay, so he didn't order you. That means you can leave the house." She smiles. "Come on, we've been cooped up for days. Let's get dressed and go. I'll call my father. He'll come and sit with Izzy so we can have some girl time. Your sister arrived last night, right? Go wake her up and tell her she's coming."

"I should show her around. She's only been to New York once before and didn't get to see much. Okay, let's do it, but we are going to be quick, and I'm sending T a message to let him know."

"You are too good for him, you know that?"

"Nope, he's a legit dream come true." I smile like the lovesick fool I am. Turning off the stove, I top the milk down the sink, excited by the prospect of Helena's coffee. I run into Bray and Reilly's guest room, and thank the heavens that I don't catch them in the act. "Rye, get up! We're going out for coffee." I throw the blanket off her. She's completely naked underneath, so I quickly pull it back up.

"Argh, go away. What kind of monster are you? Who the hell wakes people up at this ungodly hour?" Reilly groans, covering her head with the blanket.

"Come on, Rye, I want you to meet Helena. You'll love her. But you'll love her coffee more."

Her head pokes out. "Coffee? Why didn't you start with that? Give me five minutes."

"Babe, you're gonna need more than five minutes," Bray grumbles.

"Nope. No, she isn't. You can keep it in your pants for a few hours while I steal her away."

"Joke's on you, Hol. I'm not wearing any pants." Bray laughs.

"Five minutes, Rye. Be ready." I run into T's old bedroom and quickly throw on some jeans and a sweater. I pull down a pair of black boots and a white coat. Perfect. I don't have time to fix the bird's nest that is my hair, so I run a brush through it a few times, then put a beanie on to cover the mess. I look like the old me. The me before Theo. Nothing fancy, just plain old

Holly. I don't care though. I'm comfortable, and right now, that beats style any day.

I wait in the foyer and instantly regret not putting more effort into my outfit when Angelica and Reilly come bounding down the stairs. They look like they've just stepped out of Paris fashion week. Bloody hell, I really should go and change.

"Love the boots. I'm stealing them before I leave," Reilly says when she reaches me. "Okay, I was promised coffee, so let's get out of here." She links her arm with mine.

"I'll drive. Come on."

As I turn on the light to the garage, Reilly gasps. "Holy shit, Holly. This is... this is fucking epic."

I don't know what keys I picked out of the drawer. They have a numbering system, but I have no clue what it is. I'm delighted when a sleek black Maserati lights up. "Come on, I've been waiting to drive this." Reilly jumps in the passenger seat while Angelica slides in the back. When we get to the end of the drive, the guard eyes us with caution. I roll the window down and smile. "Good morning, how are you?" I ask him.

"Ma'am, the boss said no one was leaving the grounds today."

"Well, the boss ain't here, and I'm on my way out. Do I really need to call my husband and tell him one of his men is preventing me from running my daily errands?" I bat my lashes at him.

"No, of course not. Just wait here for a minute. You can't leave without protection. That's non-negotiable."

He speaks Italian into his ear piece, and moments later, a blacked-out SUV pulls up behind us. "Right, they'll follow you."

I look in the rear-view mirror. There're only two men in that car. That's fine. I can live with that. After seeing how stressed T has been, it's obvious this supposed war is really happening. I'm starting to second-guess our little outing. Maybe I should just stay in the house, like he asked.

"Nope, you are not chickening out, Holly. Let's go already." Angelica taps me on my shoulder from the back seat.

"Okay, but we are going in and out. We're not dining in. We are just getting takeaway and bringing it back," I tell them before hitting the gas.

I wait in the car until T's men step out of the SUV and are standing in front of us. I don't know why, but I have a bad feeling. It's probably just that I'm doing exactly what I promised Theo I wouldn't. I did text him though. He read my message but didn't respond, which is strange, but I'm putting that down to him being busy. "Angelica, have you spoken to Neo since he left the house this morning?" I ask her.

"No, why would I?"

"I sent T a message to tell him we were going out,

and he hasn't responded." I bite on my bottom lip. What if something's wrong?

"Holly, he's fine. He's Theo Valentino. Trust me, I used to hear stories about him all the way back in Italy."

"Yeah, you're probably right. Come on, let's go. You girls can have the coffee and I'll just inhale it—you know, pretend like I'm actually drinking it. I'll just order a hot chocolate."

"Why are you giving up coffee? You can't trust people who don't drink coffee, Hol." Reilly screws up her face.

"I'm pregnant. T said that pregnant chicks aren't meant to drink coffee," I explain, like it makes total sense.

"How the hell does he know that?" Reilly and Angelica both ask as we step out of the car.

"He read it. On Google." And, yep, I know how bad that sounds. But what if he's right? I'm not taking any chances. I won't hurt this child with caffeine or anything else I'm not meant to eat. I stop. I actually want to protect this baby. I mean, I never really thought of harming it at all or anything like that. But there's a deep need inside me to protect it. The thought has me putting a hand on my stomach.

Theo was right. Everything is going to be okay.

We've practically ordered everything on the menu. I'm kind of glad for the *no coffee* rule because even the smell is making me nauseous right now.

Helena comes out with a box full of takeaway containers. "Here you go." She hands the box to Reilly. "Hold on one sec. Your drinks are almost done. It's so freaking awesome that there are two of you, Holly. I mean, one of you is awesome, but there are two." Helena shakes her head. "It's uncanny just how identical you are."

"Yeah, we get that a lot." I'm used to the confusion. Most people can't tell us apart, whereas Bray always has a way of just knowing. We tried to fool him once. Reilly made me swap clothes with her back in the days when she was trying to avoid him. And her feelings. Suffice to say, that little song and dance did not last long. She was head over heels for the guy before she even knew it.

I've tried to pinpoint the moment I fell in love with T. The problem is I can't. I remember the chills I got the first time I heard his voice, right here, in Helena's café. I was too scared to look up and meet the face that sound belonged to. I felt *something* then... I just can't put a name as to what. I glance over at the empty sofa, the very thing that sealed my fate. The inconspicuous piece of furniture that put me in the direct path of Theo Valentino.

So much has happened since that day. Both good and bad. I wouldn't change any of it though. Well, that's not true. I'd change Italy. That event, I could live without.

"Here're your drinks." A waitress hands Angelica the tray containing four cups, and we say our goodbyes to Helena, with a promise to meet up soon.

As if karma is punishing me for today's excursion, the moment I get to the door, the nausea hits me big time. "Ah, you guys go ahead. I'm just going to run to the bathroom before we leave. I'll meet you in the car." I don't wait for a response as I power walk in the opposite direction.

Before the stall door is even fully closed, I'm bent over the toilet and tasting my dinner from last night for a second time. Geez, I really thought I was getting out of this today. "It's okay. It's not your fault." I rub my stomach. I really need to do some research and find out if he can hear me yet. *Or she.*

Flushing the toilet, I wash my hands and run some water over my face. Then I take a deep breath, cup my palms under the faucet, and rinse out my mouth. I really need to start traveling with a toothbrush if this is going to be a regular thing. As I exit the bathroom, I find the two soldiers waiting for me. "You both followed me? Who's with my sister? And my sister-in-law?" I ask.

They share a look, obviously confused. "Mrs.

Valentino, our orders are to protect you. At any and all costs."

Yeah, that's not good enough. I shake my head. "Let's just go." I storm out of the coffee shop, stopping short when I get to the sidewalk where our cars are parked. "No, no, no." I'm picked up from behind, and before I know it, I'm thrown into the back of the SUV.

"Ma'am, you need to calm down."

"Calm down! Where the fuck is my sister? Let me out! Now!" The engine shifts into gear and the vehicle takes off.

"Can't do that, ma'am. We need to get you back to the estate."

"No, I need to find her. I need to find them. Stop the fucking car!" I scream, banging at the window. "I'm going to make sure my husband tortures you slowly. In fact, I might even watch. Let me the fuck out *now*!"

"I'm sorry, ma'am. We will find them. But first, we need to get you to the estate. We need to protect you—it's protocol."

Protect me? My fucking twin sister is gone. What the fuck? I don't care about my protection. I need to find her. As soon as I can get my hands on a gun, I swear to all that is holy, I'm shooting these idiots.

Chapter Twenty-Five

I can't believe I'm in New York City. I can't believe that this is Holly's life now. She's no longer the shy, timid twin sister, following in my shadow. No, now she is a fucking queen. I couldn't be prouder of how far she has come out of her shell and into her own over the last few months. Would I have preferred that she had fallen in love with someone quiet? Safe? Like another school teacher or maybe a banker? Yes. Because then I wouldn't have to wake up bloody worrying about her every day.

I've never seen her happier though. And I would never want to take that away from her. She is my rock, my ride or die. I'll do anything for her, as she would for me. I won't forget the months she sat with me at Bray's bedside while he was in a coma. Or the way she dusted herself off and took care of me and Mum after our dad went to prison.

She's always been the stronger of us two. Most people would never believe that. They would assume that because I am the more outspoken, lively twin, I'm somehow tougher. Braver. But Holly, she's never been afraid to chase after what she wants.

And now, she has everything she's ever dreamed of. A husband, who fucking idolizes the ground she walks on. A baby on the way. Albeit, she did get more than she bargained for with this whole "my husband's a mob boss" thing she has going on.

I look up and down the street. Holly's just run into the bathroom. I can tell she's sick. I'm starting to feel nauseous myself. "I'm going to put this in the car, and I'll go check on Hol," I tell Angelica. I'm opening the door to the Maserati and that's when I feel it. Something cold and metal pressed to the back of my head. I freeze.

"Step away from the car, Mrs. Valentino. We're going to take a little trip." I nod my head, letting them think I'm my twin, while praying that she stays in that bathroom long enough to remain unseen. I turn around slowly. Angelica has a gun pointed at her head as well. She winks at me and smirks. Is she fucking crazy? Why the hell is she smirking?

We're led to a van. Yep, predictable. It's how every crazy serial killer story goes: *The girl was abducted in a white van...* I can't help but laugh when we're shoved inside and the door locks.

Angelica starts yelling something in Italian. I think I'm still in shock. Is this actually happening right now? They were going to do this to my sister... I would much rather it be me instead. "Angelica, calm down. How the hell do we get out of here?" I hiss.

"We don't. We wait. We let them take us to wherever they're taking us, and we wait. Don't worry, I won't let anything happen to you, Holly." And her lips curl again. Yep, definitely crazy...

"Right, we've been abducted at gunpoint but don't worry. Sorry, mate, it's a little fucking bloody hard not to worry right now."

"Trust me," she whispers before issuing her threats, "Do you have any idea who I am, idiots? When my father finds out about this, you'll be sorry. He won't just kill you; he'll keep you alive for months. Torture you every fucking day, until he finally gets bored of hearing you scream. Then, when he does decide to end your miserable lives, your last words will be thanking him for the final act of mercy."

A window at the front of the van opens. "Daddy can't save you now, sweetheart. Whoever the fuck your daddy is." A thick Irish accent laughs back at us.

"You don't know that I'm Angelica Donatello? That my father's Al Donatello?" She smirks as the man's face visibly pales. "Yeah, that's what I thought."

Why does her father's name incite so much fear? I thought my brother-in-law was meant to be some big-time mob boss, and these clowns clearly had no problem abducting his wife.

"He never said anything about her being a Donatello. Fuck, man, do you really wanna do this?" We don't hear the response as the window's slammed shut again. After about thirty minutes of a cold, bumpy ride, the van comes to a stop and the doors open. I have to squint as the blinding sunlight streams in.

"Out, now."

Angelica gives my hand a little squeeze as we climb out. We're greeted by some mean-looking redheaded guy.

"I've been waiting a long time to meet ya. The legendary Mrs. Valentino. The siren who hooked Theo in just a few weeks." His grimy fingers run down my face.

"The woman who's going to cut your bloody hand off if you touch me again," I yell, which only earns me a slap across the face. I can't help my knee-jerk reaction. My literal knee jerk, as my knee connects with his balls and he bends over in pain. I smirk. That'll teach him to fucking hit me.

A moment later, he's straightening. "Feisty. I'm going to love fucking the fight out of you. But not here.

Let's go say hello to your husband. I want him to watch the show before I kill the little Italian fucker."

I can't help the panic that courses through me. I don't know how the hell I will survive this. I glance to my side, and one look at Angelica puts me at ease a little. She's not worried at all. If anything, she appears... bored.

We're led into a building by the Irishman and his sore balls. I don't have to turn around to know there's a gun pointed at my head again. I can bloody feel the metal digging into my skull. Every self-defense move Bray has ever taught me runs through my mind. But am I actually good enough to pull any of them off? I don't know.

We enter a damp room, and I come face-to-face with Theo. The wild look in his eyes as they land on us doesn't last long, and something else crosses his face. Recognition. He knows I'm not Holly. Is that a good thing or not? Will he fight as hard to help *me*? What the hell am I thinking? He can't help me... He's tied to a fucking chair. Some big, tough mob boss he's meant to be.

Chapter Twenty-Six

Holly

olly

As soon as the car stops in front of the house, I'm storming through the doors, cursing the two soldiers who trail behind me. I'm on a mission. There has to be a weapon around here somewhere. I'm opening and shutting the drawers in the foyer—okay, maybe more like slamming them. I run my hands on the underside of the hall tables and then I feel it. A small gun taped to the wood paneling. I remove the tape and pray that the thing's actually loaded.

I mean, why would you tape a gun there if it wasn't loaded? Then I remember we have a kid in this house. How many more weapons are hidden around here? What if Izzy was to find one and hurt herself? Dismissing that thought for now, I point the gun at the two soldiers. To their credit, they don't even flinch.

"What the fuck is goin' on here?" Donatello's gravelly voice fills the silence.

"These incompetent idiots let my sister and Angelica get abducted and wouldn't stop to help me find them," I tell him.

"What? Who the fuck took them? The fucking Clover... I'm going to fucking skin that Irish fuck alive." Donatello puts his phone to his ear, doling out orders in rapid Italian, when Bray walks in.

"Hol, where's Reilly. What happened?"

"She... she... Someone took her, Bray. We have to find her."

"What do you mean someone took her?" His voice is cold. Calm.

"I came out of the café, and they were gone. The food was on the ground, and they were gone. I just went to the bathroom."

"Hol, where's the garage? I'm gonna need some keys."

"Where are you going?"

"I'm gonna go get my fucking wife and slit the

throats of any fucker with balls enough to touch her," he says quietly.

"How? We don't even know where she is, Bray."

He shows me his phone with a flashing light on a map. "Her ring may have a tracker in it... If you tell her, I'll deny it."

"I'm coming. Let's go."

"No, you're staying put. Trust me, Hol, I'll get her back. But I'm not taking you with me."

"I have the cars ready," Donatello adds. "Holly, I need you to stay with Izzy, please. I promise I'll take care of this."

I don't know what to do. I want to argue. I want to go with them and find my sister. And I want Theo. He'd know what to do. "Oh my God. They have T too, don't they?" All the soldiers, now standing around as if appearing from the woodwork, exchange a look but none of them answer me. These assholes have my husband and my sister. "Donatello, make them bleed. A lot," I tell him, before heading upstairs to find Izzy.

"Don't worry, I plan to."

I'm in a daze. I don't know what to do. As much as I want to go after them, I know I'll be a distraction. I'd just be in the way. But staying here, I feel useless. Helpless. What if they don't get there soon enough? What if they made Reilly remove her jewelry, and that tracker isn't leading them anywhere?

There are so many questions running through my head. I fall to the ground in the hallway. Bringing my knees to my chest, I bury my head in my thighs and let the tears fall. I don't care who sees me crying right now.

"Aunt Holly. It's going to be okay." Izzy's little hands reach out and stroke my hair. I look up into her innocent eyes.

"I'm sorry, Izzy. I'm okay. I think it's just the baby. Pregnancy makes you hormonal, you know." I try to tuck everything away.

"It's not that. I heard what Nonno was saying on the phone. Someone took my mama. And your sister. Uncle T and Neo are missing too. But it's going to be okay. Nonno will fix it. He always does," she says, and she's so bloody convincing. This little girl has seen way too much in her short life. She should be playing with dolls, toys, computer games. Instead, she's comforting me, knowing full well her mother has just been abducted.

"I'm sorry. I should have listened to your Uncle T and stayed in the house."

"Maybe. But my mama knows how to fight. No one will beat her. She's been teaching me too. She says girls need to know how to protect themselves in our world. We can't rely on boys to always save us."

"Well, your mama is a really smart woman."

"We should watch a movie. It will help pass the time. That's what I usually do when I'm waiting for things."

"That sounds like a great idea. Let's go and raid the snacks. Then we can camp out in the movie room."

"Is there a movie room in your new house, Aunt Holly?"

"There sure is."

"I think you should have a snack bar in your new house. With ice cream."

"That's a great idea."

Izzy and I snuggle up and eat our feelings away. I try to concentrate on the Disney movie she picked, but I can't help that feeling of dread. The fear that the two most important people to me are in the hands of a psycho. I need them to be okay. I need them to come back.

I try every calming technique I've ever taught my students in health and well-being class. I take deep breaths. I count forwards and backwards. I think of happy memories—except, when I do, they all include either Reilly or Theo. Which brings me back to why I'm stressed in the first place. It's been an hour. Surely, they've gotten to them by now. Why the hell hasn't anyone called?

I keep checking my phone, keep waiting for it to ring. I'd even settle for a text message telling me everything's okay and that they're on their way home. Izzy reaches out and holds my hand. I should be the one soothing her here. She's being strong, and I'm nothing but a mess.

"Do you think my mama and Neo will get married?" she questions... out of nowhere.

"I'm not sure. Why do you ask?"

"Well, Mama hasn't had a boyfriend before. And Neo makes her smile. So I like him."

"He's a good one."

"I think I'd like him to be my papa. If they get married, he'll be my stepdad. But do you think he'll let me call him Papa?"

"I'm not sure, Izzy, but I'll shoot him for you if he doesn't." I smile.

"Okay, deal. I'll ask him when he comes home," she says. Let's hope he does come home, because I'd love to see the look on his face when she asks him. "I told Mama we should move to America."

"Oh, and what did she say?"

"She said Nonno would miss us too much."

"Yeah, he probably would."

Half an hour later, the door to the movie room opens and an armed guard enters. "Ma'am, thought you'd want to know they're heading up the drive now."

"Thank you." I grab Izzy's hand and we walk out to the foyer, just as the front doors open and a heap of bodies pile in. The moment I see Reilly and Bray, I run to my sister. "Oh my God, I'm so sorry, Rye. I'm so sorry." I hug her as tight as I possibly can.

"This wasn't your fault, Hol. And I'm okay. I'm fine," she says, wiping the tears off my face.

I step back and my eyes land on Neo. He's covered in bruises... blood. I look around the crowd but I don't see Theo. "Where's my husband? Where is he?" I ask, panicked.

Why can't I see him? Why isn't he here?

Chapter Twenty-Seven

I t only takes a minute for the realization to sink in. That's not Holly. Relief washes over me before a different kind of dread takes over. Holly would never forgive me if anything were to happen to her sister. She won't be able to look at me and not blame me. I can't live in a world where Holly hates or resents me.

"Dov'è lei?" I ask Angelica. *Where is she?*

I get hit across the head. "English, fucker."

"Sicura," she responds before they can stop her. *Safe*. One word is all it takes to set me at ease.

I glance towards Neo out of the corner of my eye. My fingers are holding the rope around my wrists at the moment. I just need two minutes, and I'll have all these Irish fucks laid out. Neo has been oddly quiet since Noah Kelly (AKA The Clover) walked in with the girls. He's staring at the gun currently pointed at Angelica's head. When I look at her, she just smirks before offering a curious wink. I have a feeling this isn't the first time she's been in a situation like this.

"I'm going to enjoy watching you all burn in hell, you fucking Irish scum," Angelica hisses.

"Shut your fucking mouth." Kelly pushes her forward. "Before I have one of my men do it for you. Go sit over there and watch. It'll be your turn soon enough."

Reilly's eyes widen. She's panicked. Her face pales at what she fears is about to happen to her. I wait until Angelica is sitting on the floor; she nods at me subtly.

"You know, for a man who's about to watch his wife get used every which way possible, you're quiet, Theo. I thought the infamous Theo Valentino had more fight in him. A disappointment is what you are," Kelly grunts before grabbing Reilly around the waist.

"Oh, I'm just envisioning the many ways I'm going to rip your dirty fucking fingers off, one by fucking one. The day you thought you could touch my wife was your undoing, Kelly."

He laughs. "You believe you're in a position to stop

me? No one's coming to save you this time, Valentino. But at least you'll go out with a good show. We'll give your husband a good show, right, whore?" He grabs Reilly by the hair and shoves her down to her knees.

"Huh, I never could understand why someone would resort to selling women and children. But I get it now, why you had to do it."

"Oh, enlighten me, then. O' Great One, why is that?"

"You can't get your dick wet any other way. What woman in her right mind would want an ugly fucker like you?"

"I'm about to get my dick plenty wet, in your wife's fucking pussy, mind you." He grins before turning to Reilly. "Your husband has cost me millions of dollars! I'll be keeping you until you've worked off his debt." However, confidence is the bastard's downfall as he steps in front of my sister-in-law, his barrel no longer directed at the back of her head.

This is what I've been waiting for. There are four of them, and three of us—that is, if I'm right about my suspicions when it comes to Angelica. "Adesso," I call out as I drop the ropes from my wrists, reach down, and retrieve the knife from my ankle. Within seconds, I'm sitting upright while digging my blade into the neck of the fucker now attempting to grab for me. I shove him back, and he falls to his knees before I cut my ankles free. It all happens so quickly. Three gunshots, and then silence. I toss the knife to Neo and he follows suit, sawing at his ropes and jumping to his feet.

Reilly is on the ground, covering her head and screaming, while Angelica leans against the wall, a gun hanging loosely in her hand before she drops it to the floor. There are four bodies laid out by her feet: one still gurgling and grasping at his neck, and the other three with bullet holes through their heads.

"Fucking hell, Angelica, could have warned a guy you were a fucking assassin."

"I-It's a necessity when you're the daughter of Al Donatello." She shrugs, trying to appear unaffected. I know it's an act—a skillset I've mastered myself.

"Reilly, it's over. You're okay, sweetheart." I lift her from the ground and head towards the exit. "Let's get out of here."

She stiffens in my arms. "I'm okay. Put me down," she says. I would like to argue, but I'm fucking struggling here. My head fucking hurts like a motherfucker, and I'm fucking dizzy as shit. I slowly lower her to her feet.

"Thank you."

"You shouldn't be thanking me. You shouldn't even be here. What the fuck happened?" I ask.

"We just went to the coffee shop. I don't even know…"

"Where's Holly?"

"She's at your parents' estate." A familiar voice cuts in. I look up and see Donatello flanked by a small army of his soldiers and one pissed off Bray Williamson.

He barges forward and snatches Reilly out of my arms. "Rye, babe, look at me." He draws her chin up with the tip of his thumb and forefinger. "Who. The. Fuck. Put their hands on you?" he yells.

"I-I'm okay, Bray. Just get me out of here. Please."

"Where is he?" He doesn't answer her and instead looks to me.

"You're about two minutes too late. He's in there with what's left of his brain splattered on the walls." I point behind me, right as Neo and Angelica exit the room.

"Angelica, stai bene?" Donatello asks, not making a move.

"Sì, sto bene," she answers. *I'm fine.*

Donatello eyes her from head to toe before nodding once and aiming his glare at Neo. "I expect to see you soon." Then he turns and walks out, his men following his steps.

Neo doesn't answer. He's too busy staring at Angelica, his expression a mix of confusion and... *intrigue.*

"Babe, hold on a sec." Bray gently shoves his wife behind him, and I don't have the time or wherewithal to duck. I don't even see the fist coming my way, until after it's already connected with my jaw and tucked back against the former pro fighter's chest. It takes a moment for my brain to catch up. All I see is the ground spinning, right before my body falls.

"No, get out! You're not coming near him." I wake to Holly screaming at someone. Opening my eyes, I squint at the bright light before shutting them again.

"Holly, put the gun down," I hear Neo say.

"Make me," she counters.

"Dolcezza? Can you just shoot him already? My head fucking hurts from all this yelling."

Holly gasps. "T, you're awake. Thank God!" She springs forward and climbs on top of me. I blink as I open my eyes again, and her blurry face comes into focus. She hits my shoulder. "What the bloody hell were you thinking? You almost got yourself killed, *for real* this time."

"I had it under control." I try to placate her.

"No, you didn't. I'm never letting you out of my sight again." Tears are streaming down her face, and my heart breaks. I did this to her. Again. My life is supposed to be dedicated to making her happy, yet all I seem to do is cause her grief.

"Don't cry, dolcezza. It's okay. It's over now."

"It's really over? The war? The Clover? It's finished?"

"Yes." I look around her to see Neo, Angelica, Bray, and Reilly—all standing in the room watching our exchange. "Should I start charging for the fucking show? What the fuck are you all doing in here?"

"Well, *I* was waiting for a thank you. You know, for saving the day and all," Angelica says.

"And I was waiting for your lazy ass to wake the fuck up," Neo grunts. "Now that you have, I have more pressing matters to deal with. Angelica, let's go."

I groan as they practically run out the door. I don't even want to think about what those *pressing matters* include.

"I, ah, I want to say I'm sorry. For the hit. But I'm not. If you ever get my wife caught up in your shit again, I will fucking kill you. I don't care how many men you have standing between us," Bray says.

I take the gun out of Holly's hand just as she picks it up. "It's okay, dolcezza. He has every right to be angry." I nod at her before looking to Bray.

"Right... And just so you know, if you weren't important to Holly, you'd already be in a shallow grave," he grunts from beside his wife.

"Okay, well, now that we're all one big happy family again, let's eat. I'm starving," Reilly interjects.

"We'll be right down." Holly waits until the door shuts, then her eyes land back on me. "On a scale of one to ten, how bad does it hurt?" she asks.

"One," I lie.

"Try again."

"Ten. But it's nothing new."

"I called the doc to come and check you over. He should be here soon."

I smile wide. "You didn't have to do that. I'll be fine. I just need some Tylenol and maybe a few days in bed. With you."

"Just try to get rid of me, Theo Valentino. I'm going to be stuck to you like glue."

"Good. You know, I do hurt really bad, dolcezza. Maybe I need a sponge bath."

She grinds down on my hard cock. "Somehow, I think you're going to make a speedy recovery."

"With you taking care of me, how could I not?"

"I was really scared, T. I didn't like it. Also, we're putting an ice cream stand in our movie room in the new house."

"I'm sorry I scared you. And you can put whatever you want in the house, dolcezza."

"I love you. I'm really glad you didn't break your promise and you came back to me."

"Tornerò sempre da te. Always. I'll always come back to you, Holly."

"Always." She nods.

Epilogue

Ten years later

T

I never imagined my world would be so complete, so fucking perfect. To think I almost blindly went along with my father's plans for an arranged marriage all those years ago. Until Holly. A single glance at the woman, and I knew she'd be the one to save me. To change the trajectory of my life, for the better. And she did. She still does. Every fucking day.

While my world *is* perfect, the word doesn't come close enough to describing her. She's fucking extraordinary. I always thought God was playing some fucked-up trick: giving her to me, only to take her away again. But even heaven would have trouble prying that angel from my arms.

It took a long time to forgive my mother for hiding my biological father's identity from me. I've had a conversation with her. And although she had very valid reasons—she was a scared, young teenage girl—I still held a grudge for a while.

Thanks to Angelica and Izzy, I've managed to build somewhat of a connection with Al Donatello. Will I ever call him *Dad*? Absolutely fucking not. But my kids do refer to him as Nonno. Especially considering he and my mother are fucking married now. But that's a story for another fucking day.

I watch Theo and Matteo play ball out in the field Holly insisted they needed. A fucking football field in our backyard. You really can't get more all-American than that. She says the boys have too much pent-up energy, and the more time they spend outdoors, the better off we all are. I learned quickly that my wife is right ninety-nine percent of the time. I don't bother arguing with her on most things. She wins every time I fucking do anyway.

Romeo stumbles across the deck, attempting to climb up the railing. The one-year-old's not happy that his older brothers are out on the grass and he's not.

Ever since he could move, he's been following the older two around everywhere.

"Don't let him fall, T," Holly warns as she watches his resourcefulness at trying to make it over.

"Dolcezza, have I ever let any of them fall?" I ask, offended. I lean in, pressing my lips to her forehead before bending down and kissing Luca's tiny little head as he sleeps on Holly's chest. I can't help but want more children. Holly really does create the perfect offspring.

"You're not getting me knocked up again, T. We were meant to stop after Matteo."

"And we did, for several years," I argue. There is a six-year age gap between Matteo and the twins. Theo is the oldest of our boys; he just turned nine. Then there is Matteo, who's seven. Romeo and Luca came as a surprise six years later. "Maybe we should just try for one more. Fifth one might be a girl," I suggest.

"Not a bloody chance in hell, T. You can keep your... *thing* well and clear away from me." Holly glares in my direction.

I bend down and pick up the rebellious one-year-old. "You'd like a little sister, wouldn't you, Romeo?" I put his mouth to my ear. "What was that? Yes?" I smirk at my wife. "See? He wants a sister. How can you say no to this face?" I ask.

"I have a feeling a lot of girls are going to have trouble saying no to that face. But I won't be one of them."

"We'll work on her," I tell him.

"Ma'am, dinner is ready." Rosa pokes her head out the door. Holly was resistant to the idea of having a cook at first, but I want to make things as easy as possible for her. Also, her Italian cooking skills are practically nonexistent, not that I'll ever admit that to anyone.

"Thank you, Rosa. T, get those two to come in and wash up."

"Theo! Matteo! Dinner's ready. Come on inside."

"Dad, did you see that tackle? I think I almost broke him," Theo says, pulling his younger brother to his feet.

"Shake it off, Matteo. You'll be fine." Am I hard on my children? Not at all. But, unlike my wife, I also don't wrap them up in cotton wool. I think she forgets the world we live in sometimes.

When I look at these boys, part of me hopes they never want to follow in my footsteps. That they go off to college and lead normal lives—well, as normal as possible, given their gene pool. Then, there's another part that wants one of them to carry on our family legacy. Both the legitimate and the not-so-legitimate innerworkings. Over the years, with Holly's assistance, our above-board earnings are almost matching those we take in from our... *other* ventures. My wife is fucking smart and has a mind for business and investments. Her advice has never steered me wrong.

"Don't worry, Dad. Next time, I'll duck quicker." Matteo runs up to me.

"Good. Make sure you do. Never let anyone get the better of you."

"Never," he parrots, sprinting past me.

"Theo, wait up." I stop my eldest in his tracks. "You need to be looking out for your brothers, not fucking hurting them. There are plenty of other people in our world who will want to do just that: hurt them, inflict pain, bring one or all of you down. You boys are always on the same team, got it?"

"Got it, Dad. It's just a game. Don't worry, I'll always protect them. No matter what, right?" Theo says.

"No matter what," I repeat the phrase we've always told each other. *Family comes first. Always. No matter what.* "Come on, don't keep your mother waiting."

Epilogue

Holly

Everyone is sitting around the dinner table. My heart hurts with how much love is in this room. How my whole world is around this dinner table. I was once worried I wouldn't be able to love anyone as much as I loved my husband, not even our own child.

But that fear was baseless. I fell in love with our

little Theo as soon as I let myself relax and embrace the idea of becoming a mother. When he was born and placed on my chest, I cried tears of joy. He was so tiny, a head full of dark hair. So fragile and so bloody perfect. I've never wanted to wrap something up and hide it—hide *them all*—away from the world so badly before. If I could lock us in a vault and never have to face the dangers of outside, I would.

That's no life for a child though. I've worked hard on dealing with my anxieties and overbearing mothering over the years. I want my kids to experience everything this world has to offer. I want them to be boys and explore. But I also want them to be safe... to never feel pain.

Did I used to freak out and call the doctor every time Theo scraped his knees, or hit his head on something when he was a toddler? Yes, I might have. But to his credit, the doctor humored me and always came to check him over.

By the time Romeo came along, I've pretty much eased a lot of those worries. I know kids fall, scrape knees, lose teeth, etc. But I would appreciate it if Romeo and Luca would just take life a little less rough than what Theo and Matteo seem to. Those two are always getting into scrapes at school. T says it's normal for boys to fight. I think he forgets that I used to be a teacher at one point in time. And it's *not normal* to be called up to the school every other week because your third-grader (or your first-grader) has beaten up another student. They're always tight-lipped too. Never really give much of a reason as to why they started a fight, except that the other person deserved it.

"So, either of you want to explain what happened at school today?" I ask, pointing my fork between the two of them. They look at each other, then back to me without a single word. "No? Because, from what I heard from Principal Wendy, you both attacked that boy."

"Principal Wendy is a bitch," Theo grumbles.

T coughs into his hand, attempting to hide his laughter, as I send daggers his way. "What? He's not fucking wrong."

"That's not the point. Theo, you don't call women *bitches*. Ever! It's rude."

"What about female dogs? They're called bitches."

"We're not talking about dogs, Theo. We're talking about why you two thought it was okay to beat up another boy today."

"Pity, I'd rather talk about dogs," he groans.

"Theo, stop being a smartass to your mother and answer her questions. Apologize first." T's using his *no nonsense, don't even bother arguing with me* tone.

"Sorry, Mom. We thought it was okay to beat him up because he kissed Savvy on the mouth when she didn't want him to."

Savvy is Matteo's best friend from school. They're an odd match. She's quiet, withdrawn, shy. Whereas Matteo seems to have taken on the role of the class-bloody-clown.

"Oh, okay." I'm at a loss as to how to approach this.

On one hand, I don't want to approve of violence. But on the other, they defended the girl, which I'm absolutely proud of.

"You guys did good. Always stand up for girls. Never walk by and ignore anyone who mistreats a girl," T says, high-fiving them both. The two boys glow under his praise.

"Your father's right. How is Savannah?" I ask Matteo.

"She's fine. I brought her some candy." He shrugs.

This is my life now, navigating my way through parenting four boys, who no doubt will continue to get themselves into trouble as they grow into men. And I wouldn't change any of it for the world.

Do you still need more of Theo and Holly? Get your bonus Epilogue here - The Valentino Empire, Bonus Epilogue

Curious as to who the rat was and how the Valetinos handled the betrayal? Check out Neo and Angelica's story. Brutal Princess

Acknowledgments

Holly and Theo's journey is finished! What a ride it's been. I have laughed, cried, and screamed while making this story come to life. Not to mention, the severe RSI because I just couldn't type the words quick enough! Theo and Holly really wanted their story heard!

There are so many people I want and need to thank for assisting me and encouraging me in bringing this story to life.

Firstly, my beta readers: Aimee, Sam, Natasha, and Mel. You girls are literally the best thing since sliced bread! I love how invested you are in this story, how much time and effort you put into reading and answering my many questions, soothing my doubts, and indulging my out-there plot ideas. Thank you for being on this journey with me.

Kat, my extremely organized and amazing editor: I know I work you close to deadlines, then push the friendship boundaries by being late for said deadlines, but I could not do this without you. You are the glitter to my ordinarily plain paper!

Michelle, the amazingly talented photographer, who subbed as a cover designer for me for this trilogy: I can't even begin to express how grateful I am for all of your help on these covers. It had been my dream to have a Michelle Lancaster original on one of my covers since I discovered you in early 2021. I can now tick that off my bucket list.

About Kylie Kent

Kylie made the leap from kindergarten teacher to romance author, living out her dream to deliver sexy, always and forever romances. She loves a happily ever after story with tons of built-in steam.

She currently resides in Perth, Australia and when she is not dreaming up the latest romance, she can be found spending time with her three children and her husband of twenty years, her very own real-life instant-love.

Kylie loves to hear from her readers; you can reach her at: author.kylie.kent@gmail.com

Visit Kylie's website and sign up for her newsletter at: www.kyliekent.com

Printed in Great Britain
by Amazon